KU-314-751

Fire in the Sea

Miguel and his father leave their Spanish estates to join the great and glorious Armada. They see themselves as liberators, coming to save the long-suffering people of England from their evil, heretical Queen. But instead of being welcomed by cheering crowds, they are greeted by cannon-fire and a terrifying display of English seamanship.

Wind, weather, and English warships drive the Spanish fleet northwards to destruction. Miguel is cast ashore on the coast of Ireland. He finds that the trials he has endured are as nothing to the dangers that await him.

In *Fire in the Sea* we see the "Invincible" Armada through Spanish eyes, not as an historic English victory but as a failure of hopes and a shattering of illusions.

Fire in the Sea

AUDREY BUTLER

Blackie: Glasgow and London

Copyright© 1975 Audrey Butler
Map copyright© 1975 Blackie and Son Limited

ISBN 0 216 90117 0

Blackie and Son Limited
Bishopbriggs, Glasgow G64 2NZ
5, Fitzhardinge Street, London W1H 0DL

Printed in Great Britain by
Thomson Litho Ltd., East Kilbride, Scotland

CONTENTS

For all six of you—who have been very patient!

Fire in the Sea

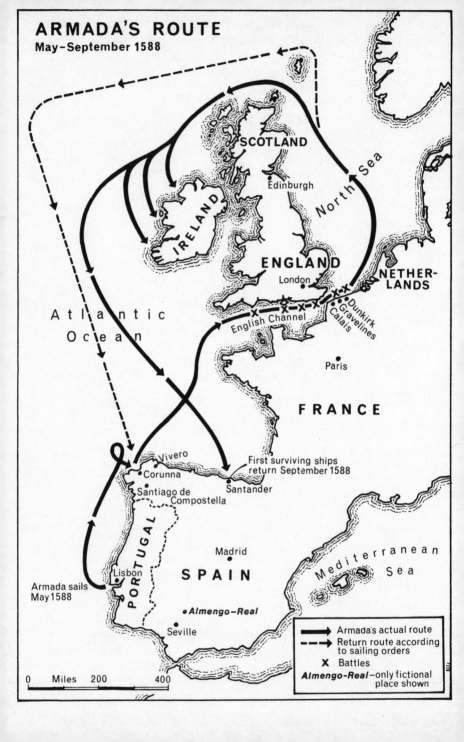

King Philip of Spain to the Duke of Medina Sidonia, February 1588:
The cause being the cause of God, you will not fail.

Copy of the Duke of Medina Sidonia's instructions for the Armada's return to Spain, August 1588:
Take great heed lest you fall upon the island of Ireland, for fear of the harm that may happen to you upon that coast.

Sir William Fitzwilliam, Lord Deputy of Ireland, to Sir Francis Walsingham, Elizabeth I's Secretary of State, referring to the wreck of the GIRONA, 28 October 1588 (Old Style)—i.e. 7 November 1588:
Since it hath pleased God, by His hand, upon the rocks, to drown the greater and better sort of them, I will, with His favour, be His soldier for the despatching of those rags which yet remain.

King Philip of Spain to his bishops and archbishops, 13 October 1588:
We are bound to give praise to God for all things which He is pleased to do. I on the present occasion have given thanks to him for the mercy which He has shown. In the foul weather and violent storms to which the Armada has been exposed, it might have experienced a worse fate...

Medallion struck to commemorate England's defeat of the Armada, 1588:
Jehovah flavit et dissipati sunt... GOD BLEW AND THEY WERE SCATTERED...

CHAPTER ONE

The News from Madrid

Miguel stirred in his sleep, half-opened his eyes. Blinding white pin-points of sunlight danced on to the bed through the gaps in the shutters; the dark, airless room rippled unsteadily around him. Although it was barely April, the days were already getting very hot. During the hours when the sun was at its highest, everyone and everything—from princes to peasants, from dukes to donkeys—retired thankfully into the shelter of castle, cottage, or the nearest olive-grove to rest until the worst of the heat was past. *La siesta*. It was a national Spanish institution, almost an obligation, coming, in Miguel's mind, into virtually the same category as Mass on Sundays.

Yet here was someone breaking it with a vengeance! He could hear the scuff of horses on the winding stone track that led up the lower slopes of the Almengo mountain from the valley below; the murmur of voices drifted on ahead.

"Father!" Of course—it could only be Father—back already from visiting the King in Madrid—and back well before the vital date of Holy Week that he had faithfully promised Mother before he left! Wide-awake now, trembling with anticipation, Miguel swung himself to his feet. As always on waking, his left leg was especially stiff and unmanageable; he half-hopped to the castle window and flung open the shutters with a yell of excitement, just in time to see his father ride out from under the main archway into the cobbled courtyard beneath him. Don Luis looked up, grinned, and threw his plumed, dust-covered hat high into the air.

"Catch!" he roared, exuberant as ever, even at the end of his two-hundred-mile, week-long journey—and, as Miguel almost toppled out of the window in the effort: "Hurry along down with it! I've brought back some wonderful news!"

For more than a year now, Spain's King Philip had been assembling the biggest and most powerful fleet the world had ever seen, with the sole aim of invading and crushing forever his arch-enemy, England. It was more than time to make it plain that his mighty Spanish Empire was sick of having her treasure-ships looted, her colonies in the Indies sacked—even home-ports like Cadiz set on fire by one cheeky little upstart nation in the North, which had set its face against the true faith, and whose rascally Queen Elizabeth employed an admiral called Drake—*el Draque*, the Dragon—who was assuredly the Devil's own son!... Victory was a foregone conclusion, of course, for right and might were on the Spanish side; and from every town and village in Spain, and from her great overseas empire, too, men were now hurrying towards Lisbon, eager to join the invincible Armada. People said it was like the age of the Crusades all over again, with the air so heady with hope and faith!

All winter, Miguel's father had fretted on his estates, and talked continually of volunteering; but his wife, less certain than most that Spain's victory really *was* assured, had always managed to dissuade him. Until last month. On hearing then that the fleet's new commander was the Duke of Medina Sidonia, a near-neighbour and old friend, Don Luis had finally swept aside all Doña Inez's arguments and even her tears and rushed off to Madrid to offer his services to the King. After he had gone, Mother's anger and distress had quickly evaporated. She had shrugged her shoulders.

"The King will not want him," she declared flatly. "After all, he has no experience of such matters. It is a touch of spring madness, nothing more. A man of thirty-eight, acting like a young lad! It is quite ridiculous! But I am afraid the refusal will hurt his pride...." And she bit her lip, and had not mentioned the matter again. Nevertheless, over the past month, there had been many times when she had been vague, irritable, not at all her usual serene self. And Father's greeting, reflected Miguel, as he limped out on to the cobbles, had certainly not been that of a man returning from a wasted journey. What in the world was Mother going to say now?

Suddenly, the courtyard was buzzing with activity. Servants appeared to lead away the horses, and to bring out pitchers of cool wine for the Count and his retinue. Don Luis enveloped Miguel in a gigantic bear-hug of an embrace, tried—apparently unsuccessfully—to lift him from the ground, and then held his son at arm's length. "Don't ever complain again that you're not growing! See—in less than a month—I can no longer lift you! And I'll swear you've added at least another inch!"

Miguel fidgeted uneasily. He loved his father passionately; yet he always felt slightly uncomfortable in his company. For the Count of Almengo-Real was everything that Miguel was not, but would have liked to be—strong, handsome, superbly self-confident.... What a disappointment it must be for him to have a son with a lame leg, who was slight and shy and forever lost in his day-dreams! Not that Don Luis had ever hinted anything of the kind, but Miguel had caught the servants whispering and sighing now and then—and if

15

servants were ashamed of the future Count of Almengo-Real—how much more so must the present Count be!

Father gave him a hearty thump on the back. "Wake up! Have you lost your tongue while I was in Madrid?"

Miguel gulped, determined for once to say the right thing, and not to stammer. "So, the news is good——" he began, hesitantly.

Don Luis let out a bellow of delight. "Good? Indeed it is—and not simply for me alone——"

Then he stopped in mid-sentence, as he saw his wife hurrying towards him across the cobbles. Doña Inez was wearing her newest gown of pale lemon silk, and the Sanchez necklace of Mexican emeralds sparkled at her throat. The veiling on her jet-black hair was caught in a velvet cap that shimmered with seed-pearls; she was smiling—her special, secret smile that was Father's alone —and Miguel thought for the thousandth time that she must be the most beautiful woman in the world. Don Luis clearly thought so, too, for he let go of Miguel's arm, and bounded towards her, about to smother her in an embrace at least as violent as the one which Miguel had just experienced. But Mother held out her arm, stiffly, so that her husband had to be content with bowing low and kissing her hand very correctly and formally.

"I'm not at court, now," he grumbled, while Doña Inez's shoulders shook with suppressed laughter. Miguel sensed she was very confident—confident that the news Father had brought back would be the rejection she had been hoping for all along. He felt himself flush miserably; there was a sick feeling in the pit of his stomach as he waited for her to be disappointed.

"So...." Mother's voice was filled with happy expectation. "You have kept your promise—and you are back in good time for Holy Week——"

Each and every year, Miguel's parents travelled to Seville for the pomp and grandeur of the Holy Week processions there. It was a sentimental journey for them, because Don Luis had first seen Mother as she watched one such procession from her father's window, and had determined there and then, without even knowing who she was, that he would marry her. Ever since then, the Count and his wife had never missed returning for the anniversary of that first meeting. As a small boy, Miguel had loved hearing his mother recount the story. It was as romantic as a fairy-tale—the poverty-stricken young nobleman falling in love at first sight with a beautiful stranger—and finding he had collected a fortune into the bargain! For in sixteenth-century Spain marriages were generally arranged without love playing any part in the matter at all—and noblemen, however poor, did not often marry merchants' daughters, however rich.

"Inez. . . ." Father's face was suddenly very solemn. "I am truly sorry—but there will be no Holy Week for us in Seville this year." He took a deep breath, then spoke with quiet, unaccustomed deliberation. "I am joining the Armada at once, for the ships are expected to sail soon after Easter and—Inez—" he faltered slightly, almost as if anticipating his wife's reaction— "I intend taking Miguel with me!"

Mother caught her breath sharply. "God have mercy! You cannot be serious! Not Miguel, too!" Her face was suddenly drained of all its colour; she was trembling, violently. Father put his arm round her shoulder, trying to steady her, but she pushed him brusquely away. For a long, embarrassing moment, no one did or said anything. The servants gaped and shuffled their feet. At last Doña Inez lifted her head. She was still deathly pale, but, surprisingly, she sounded her usual composed self once more. "You surprised me, Luis—I should not have acted so. Please forgive me." She rested her hand on her husband's arm, tried to smile. "After such a ride in the midday sun, you must be exhausted!" she said lightly, though Miguel thought he could detect a catch in her voice. "This is a shameful welcome, indeed! Come, you must have fresh clothes, and something to eat and drink, and rest . . . talking can come later, much later . . ."

Before she disappeared into the castle, Mother turned, and gave Miguel a long, wild, agonized look. It was as though she were begging him to help her change Father's mind . . . Miguel tried not to meet her eyes. He wanted her to be happy, of course; but he had just heard the most thrilling news of his life! On this great adventure—Father actually wanted him with him! Despite everything—his limp, his stammer—everything! Suddenly he felt himself a different person.

He shut his eyes ecstatically. Why, by midsummer he and Father would be riding triumphant through the streets of London; he pictured the flags, the banners, the cheering welcome of all those ordinary English folk who were said to be longing for the Spaniards to come and help them overthrow their evil, heretic Queen! Come the autumn, they would sail home again, everybody's heroes; and then how stupid Mother's gloomy forebodings would seem!

But Doña Inez did not give in so easily. Later that evening, Miguel had to stand by, silent and embarrassed, while his parents argued as he had never heard them argue before.

"You would be of more use to Spain here, looking after your estates!" cried Mother, scathingly. "What experience have you of battles—let alone of battles at sea? At your age, it is the sheerest folly! You are not a young *caballero* any more, free to go where you please and do as your fancy takes—but a great landowner and the head of a family . . ."

Father refused to be ruffled. He was the same age as the Duke of Medina Sidonia, the leader of the expedition, after all—and no one was suggesting that the Duke was too old! And he could use a sword and lead his men into action with the best of them, he went on—and besides, there would be scarcely any real fighting, for the English would most likely turn tail and run for it when they saw how powerful the Armada was!

"Our task is merely to sail up the English Channel and link up with the Duke of Parma's army, waiting in the Netherlands, and help ferry it across to England," he explained patiently. "Then we shall march on London alongside Parma's men and leave a Viceroy and a garrison in charge there. Why, we should be home in time for the wine-harvest!" Don Luis smiled, and added, jokingly— "And I promise you a fine English estate, as some compensation for missing our Holy Week together this year!"

But the jest misfired. Mother stamped her foot. "We have no need of any English estates!" Then she sighed. "What quarrel have we with England? Why, my family traded with the English for years, and they were fair in business. Both our countries benefited, I have often heard my father say so."

At this echo of his merchant father-in-law's almost treasonable ideas Father's temper finally snapped. "While your relations were busy at home, making their fortunes, my ancestors were fighting and dying to make Spain a safe and great enough place for them to do it in!" he thundered. "For over three hundred years the Counts of Almengo-Real have always gone to war when their kings required it! Oh, I grant you—it did

19

not bring them riches, like the Sanchezes, but it brought them honour!" He stopped, cut short by his wife's stricken face, and then went on, more gently. "I am sorry. That was very unfair. I owe your family my fortune—and I know they have served Spain well enough in their own way, but, can you not see? This is something I *have* to do! If I do not follow my conscience now, I shall not rest easy on my lands again!"

Mother said nothing for a moment. "I would never try to hold you against your will. I know how important this is to you. Only—" and she looked intently at her husband, and Miguel saw the silent tears streaming down her cheeks, "Being only a merchant's daughter, I am not ashamed to admit I am afraid . . . for I truly believe the English are much more stubborn and dangerous than the King realizes. . . ."

So Father had won, as he always did, and as Miguel had known that he would, in the end. Doña Inez could refuse her husband nothing. Not even their only son. All in vain she pleaded that Miguel at least should stay behind; he was too young, and then there was his leg— but Don Luis laughed away all her objections.

"He is thirteen, almost a man! It was King Philip himself who suggested that he should come with me! As for that bit of a limp—it's but a small thing, as you know in your heart, made too important by all our coddling! Haven't the doctors themselves said that his leg was only weakened by the fever—that there's no real harm done—that it's simply confidence in himself that Miguel needs now? And how better to gain it, than on this glorious adventure!" He sighed expansively. "Why, at his age I would have given my right arm for a chance such as this! For 1588 is going to be a year which the whole world will never forget!"

Doña Inez bowed her head then, finally beaten. In the

months to come, Miguel would often recall, with pain, how withdrawn she had become during those last few days. But at the time, there was so much to do, so many things to prepare, that he scarcely noticed. His extrovert father noticed even less.

Then, almost before he realized it, Miguel was astride his black Arab mare on the cobbles below the window from which, only a week earlier, he had looked out to see his father riding in with the news that had changed his whole life. Father was there beside him. There were a dozen of the Count's best tenants, too, all fine fighting-men; and double as many servants again—because no Spanish nobleman worth his salt ever went anywhere without an enormous retinue, whether or not he really needed it. Everyone was in his finest clothes for the occasion; Miguel had on a new suit of crimson velvet, and the plumes in his hat rivalled those in Father's for size!

The family's chaplain pronounced his final blessing. Then Doña Inez stepped forward, very cool and stately. She kissed Miguel formally on both cheeks; though she appeared so calm, he could feel her lips trembling, like butterfly's wings.

Then she turned to Father. Now her smile was less certain, and her eyes shone like wet stars. She slipped a slim gold ring on to her husband's finger. "If my love alone could protect you, Luis," she whispered fiercely, "then you would be truly invincible! For, truly—I have given you so much—I have nothing more left to give!"

The ring was very delicately wrought, with a tiny hand, clasping a heart, and, inscribed upon it, the words Doña Inez had just spoken: "*No tengo mas que darte* . . . I have nothing more to give you."

On impulse, Don Luis leapt down from his horse, holding his wife in one last, long, public embrace;

throwing all rules of Spanish etiquette to the winds—
and this time, Doña Inez did not try to stop him. Then,
almost reluctantly, so it seemed to Miguel, he gave the
signal for the procession to move off.

The front rider carried high the standard of the
Counts of Almengo-Real; the brightly-coloured
banner fluttered out proudly as it caught the breezes on
the open hillside. Down the winding track the riders
went, the horses picking their way among the stones;
at the very back, five little donkeys, almost invisible
beneath their heavy loads of baggage, struggled to keep
up.

Far below them, the valley was spread out in the
sun, like a picture. From this height, toy houses seemed
to huddle around toy fields, and even the great river
Guadalquivir looked no more than a silver stream,
slipping down to the sea. In the distance, Miguel
fancied he could just made out the tall spires of Seville.
Bells were ringing from every church and monastery
for miles around, sounding a Godspeed to the Count
and his son—and besides, it was Palm Sunday.

"We should be almost in earshot of the bells of Lisbon
by Easter," said Father, "And come August, and
Assumption Day, it will be those of London we'll be
hearing! But nothing will sound half as sweet as these
same Spanish bells when we return in the autumn—
and they'll all peal ten times louder then than they are
doing today, even, I'll wager!"

Miguel nodded, smiling broadly. He felt ready to
explode with happiness. It was moving and exciting at
one and the same time, being in a procession like this.
He felt part of a carnival and yet part of a pilgrimage
as well. All the way down the hillside, people were
waiting to wave and cheer; girls scattered leaves and
petals in front of them. They might have been returning

victorious already, instead of merely setting out on the first stage of their great adventure!

The sun rimmed the landscape in a halo of palest gold, as if Heaven had come down to touch them; the whole world seemed to be wishing them well. Miguel's spirits soared to heights of dizzy ecstasy; how lucky he was to be alive at such a time, when life was so wonderful and so full of promise!

Then he glanced back, up the mountain, and saw the people from the castle, standing outside the outer wall, still waving their goodbyes. He could even make out his mother, like a dart of sunlight in her lemon gown, and he knew that, although she was smiling and waving with the rest, her heart was near to breaking. And, for a fleeting moment, he wished more than anything that he could turn in his tracks and make once more for the safety and shelter of the castle before it was too late.

CHAPTER TWO

"The Most Happy Armada"

But this feeling quickly vanished, returning only fitfully, now and then, in the twilight times between sleeping and waking, when the truth always seems at its most inescapable. For the cheering and the waving went with them all along their journey; sometimes Miguel felt that the tide of goodwill was physically carrying them along, it was so intense. And in such an atmosphere, any lingering doubts or regrets were all too easily pushed aside and forgotten.

They reached Lisbon just after Easter. It was raining when they arrived; a chill wind was blowing in from the Atlantic. Lisbon teemed with the thousands who had come either to join in or make money out of the Armada enterprise; the narrow streets were packed with jostling people shouting in half the languages of Europe —for at this time Spanish rule extended not merely over Spain alone, but over Flanders, Portugal and much of Italy, too—quite aside from the vast new Empire in the Americas.

The rain, the crowds, the nauseating stench from the harbour—Miguel forgot them all, as he caught his first glimpse of the mighty fleet they had come to join, riding proudly at anchor. Scores and scores of ships of every size and shape, stretching away in ordered ranks into the far horizon—everything from tall, graceful galleons to the humblest little transport hulks. Father was right! There could indeed be no greater honour on this earth than to be a part of such a marvellous venture! Why, he almost pitied the English—faced with this, they were obviously beaten even before the battle had begun!

But, to his surprise, at the Viceroy's palace—the Armada's headquarters—by contrast, everything seemed in utter confusion. The corridors buzzed with officials, soldiers, sea-captains and the like, all apparently out of sorts and full of complaints. There was no one in overall charge. Don Luis' request to see the Duke of Medina Sidonia simply led to him and Miguel being passed from clerk to clerk. Very soon, the Count became exceedingly angry.

So, to the sixth hapless official to whom he had been directed, he fairly spat out the words: "For the last time—I am Luis, fourteenth Count of Almengo-Real—and I demand to see the Duke *now*, not next week, or the week after——"

At this, a tall, fair, youngish man, even taller than Don Luis, stepped out from the press of people, and swept the Count a flourishing bow. "Don Luis! I am delighted to make your acquaintance! For you are to be on my ship——" and he bore an astonished Father and Miguel off to an empty window-seat. "*I* will personally take you to the Duke," the stranger continued, "but first, let me introduce myself! My name is Alonso Martinez de Leyva—His Majesty has entrusted me with a whole shipload of young men for this expedition—I believe I must have been given charge of at least one son from every great family in Spain! Oh, they will make first-class soldiers, but—" he smiled, deprecatingly, "they are too much for me to handle alone! Such a boisterous troupe badly needs a leaven of older men—with stability, common sense—like you, Don Luis..."

At the name of Alonso de Leyva Miguel had almost

jumped from his seat with excitement. For de Leyva was famous throughout Spain—brave, handsome, and a brilliant general, he had made a name for himself in Italy and Flanders, and was a byword for courage and chivalry, and every boy's hero, including Miguel's.... But he had never expected to see his hero in the flesh, let alone sail with him! "It's too good to be true!" he breathed, scarcely conscious that he was speaking aloud.

Both men laughed. Don Alonso held out his hand to Miguel. "Come—as the *Rata's* youngest volunteer so far—the *Rata* is the name of my ship—take my arm, and you and your father shall come with me to the Duke, so that all this business may be entered in triplicate in some clerk's little ledger, and sent off to Madrid. Why—" and he shot Father a meaningful glance—"If filling in papers could win a battle, there would be no need for us to leave port—the tons of parchment and gallons of ink that have been devoted to this affair defy description!"

"And yet I believe the King reads every word that's sent him," responded Father, carefully, as they set off along the corridor.

"I don't doubt it—and writes as much again in return—no wonder everything moves so slowly—I sometimes think the pen is almost as much of a threat to Spain as *el Draque* himself!" said Don Alonso, half-jokingly. "However—in spite of everything—we really *are* almost ready, now! Indeed, Don Luis, you have only just arrived in time! The day after tomorrow, there is to be a special High Mass in the cathedral here, when the Armada standard will be solemnly consecrated—and then we shall all board ship. Think of it—after all these delays—we could be on our way to England within the week!"

Minutes later, Miguel and his father were being

ushered into the commander-in-chief's study, and Don Alonso had gone. Without him, everything suddenly seemed much less positive again.

Not that the Duke of Medina Sidonia was unwelcoming. He hurried forward, smiling, embraced them both warmly, called for wine to be brought, and then plunged straight into a series of questions about day to day life in Andalusia.

"Was the weather fine, when you left? Were the orange-flowers budding? How were the vines shaping——?"

Father burst out laughing. "I did not come all this way simply to talk about farming!"

The Duke sighed. He looked worn and harassed. "I am sorry, Luis—but it has been raining almost perpetually since I arrived here—people say they have never known such a dreadful spring! If it's been doing the same at Sanlucar, my oranges and grapes will be ruined——"

"Don't worry!" Father grinned. "The weather was perfect when we left Almengo—why, you will be going home to a bumper harvest, as well as to a hero's welcome!"

Medina Sidonia shook his head, dolefully. "I wish I could believe you...oh, the harvest may be safe enough, but as to the rest...." He hesitated, then burst out: "There is still so much to do you see, but we cannot afford to wait any longer...there aren't enough cannon, and the shot is poor, and the food is already going bad in the barrels...then there are the problems of mixing the different nationalities—the Italians are quarrelling with the Spaniards who are quarrelling with the Portuguese who are of course quarrelling with everyone....On top of it all, His Majesty keeps sending me more and more instructions—

look—" he shuffled miserably with an enormous pile of papers on his desk, "dealing with everything under the sun. I am being smothered beneath a mountain of royal paper—and torn apart by arguing commanders. The King has picked some fine men to help me—but most of them cannot agree among themselves except to make it abundantly clear that they think very little of *me*—and who can blame them?" He ran his hands wildly through his hair. "I never wanted to lead this enterprise! I begged the King not to give me the command—I'm not a professional soldier or sailor and I detest the sea . . . all I want to do is to get back to my orange-groves——"

"Come now, de Leyva seems confident enough—except about the mountains of paper!" Though Don Luis' voice was cheerful, Miguel sensed that his Father had been thoroughly taken aback by the Duke's outburst—the more so, because, in the past, Medina Sidonia had always seemed such a mild, placid person, whom nothing could ruffle. And he felt a sudden stab of pain as he remembered Mother waving goodbye to them, and the pain turned momentarily to apprehension as he recalled those brief seconds of appalling doubt . . .

"De Leyva? Ah—but he is a born hero—he makes the best of everything!" The Duke actually managed a half-smile. "He is to command the Spanish armies, once we land in England, you know—a splendid fellow —but some of the others are more trouble than they are worth . . . I confess, I'm at my wits' end——"

Father raised his goblet; Miguel knew that he was heartily sick of listening to the Duke's interminable tale of woe. "Let us at least drink to our success in England," he said, very firmly. "Of one thing, at least, I am quite convinced there's no argument—the final outcome!" He jogged Miguel's elbow. "Come, Miguel, you too!

To the success of our Armada—what was it King Philip called it? Ah, yes—*la felicissima Armada*—the most happy Armada—let us drink to that!"

"The most happy Armada!" echoed the Duke. "Let us hope she lives up to her name!" But his voice had a strangely cynical ring, as if he had no real faith in what he was saying.

Then it was April 25th, St Mark's Day. The day chosen for the Armada battle-standard's solemn consecration.

All his life long, Miguel would remember this day. Lisbon cathedral was ablaze with candles; its altars decorated with their richest hangings and jewels. On the great high altar lay the Armada banner itself. Then the Archbishop stepped forward to begin the Mass. The well-known, well-loved words echoed the length and breadth of the vast building; the responses from the massed choirs soared heavenwards in a mighty shout of triumph. The very air seemed to crackle with spiritual fervour; the congregation was inspired, and Miguel with it!

He felt himself strong as a lion, invincible as the Armada itself, protected by the absolute certainty that God was on his side. There were no doubts or fears any more; he shut his eyes, and prayed, fervently. He prayed for success for God and for Spain. And he prayed—a little reluctantly—that the wretched English would see the error of their ways and return to the faith of their forefathers. In his present state of hysterical conviction they had become in his mind very different from the fair-minded trading partners that his Grandfather Sanchez talked of so nostalgically. Now he saw them as grotesque, misshapen, larger than life—but all bearing the grinning, hideous features he had come to associate with the dreaded *el Draque*, the English admiral, Francis Drake himself! Nothing could save them now, however. Even Drake would soon be no more than an evil memory, when the Heaven-sent Armada had swept the seas clear of him and all his kind!

The Mass ended as triumphantly as it had begun; the sacred banner was borne out into the sunshine, the congregation following. Miguel watched it being carried through the packed lines of kneeling soldiers and sailors, back to the Duke's flagship, ready for hoisting when the vital battle should begin.

In the harbour, every ship in the fleet was flying its flags and banners. There were sixty-five galleons assembled there, the pride of Spain's navy—handsome sailing vessels that had already proved their practical excellence on the Atlantic voyages between Spain and the Indies. In addition to all these there were four massive galleys which relied for their power on rowers alone—convicts or Moslem prisoners-of-war captured in Mediterranean battles with Turkish and Arab pirates, and in any case no better than slaves—as well as four enormous, cumbersome galleasses, which were powered by a combination of rowers and sails. The galleons would be the spearhead of the Spanish attack; the galleys and galleasses were intended for ramming the English ships so that the enemy could be boarded and then overpowered in pitched battles fought on the decks—the classic Spanish idea of a sea-battle. Then there were nearly sixty other boats to carry all the extra stores—horses, shot and the like. Though some of these were quite large, others were little more than fishing smacks, converted into supply hulks for the occasion. No English navy, however valiant, however confident, could possibly hope to withstand this mighty Armada of over one hundred ships and thirty thousand men!

All the bells of Lisbon were pealing; from the water-front came the roar of salvo upon salvo of ships' cannon. The sky was a hard, steely blue, and from it, sharp as a Toledo sword, a brilliant sun beat down upon the rows of bowed heads, and upon the dazzling banner itself.

The bells chimed, the guns boomed. The intensity of sound seemed to shake all Lisbon to its very foundations; the great flag, the kneeling masses around it, quivered and shook as if seen through a kind of distorting mirror. There was a dull drumming in Miguel's ears; he felt dizzy, almost drunk with pent-up emotion.

"Arise, O Lord, and Make Your Cause Succeed!" the banner proclaimed. Of course—for how could it fail? Even the melancholy Duke seemed transformed by today's great ceremony—confident and smiling, his doubts vanished! As for Miguel—he felt as if the whole world lay already at his triumphant feet!

CHAPTER THREE

Into the Channel!

Two months later, however, when the Armada had still not sighted England, much of the heady, unquestioning enthusiasm of St Mark's Day had been dissipated by a series of frustrations and disappointments.

From the outset, the Spanish fleet had been dogged by bad luck. A violent onshore wind kept it penned inside Lisbon harbour until the end of May, and when it did reach the open sea a gale promptly blew it in quite the wrong direction, so that it actually came within sight of North Africa! Then the weather turned hot and sultry, and the Armada was almost becalmed. Food and water ran short, epidemic sickness swept the fleet, and everyone's temper reached breaking-point. So a tempest which forced it to put in to Corunna, in north-east Spain, early in July, turned out to be something of a godsend, even though the damage it did was considerable. For while repairs were being carried out, there was time, too, to replenish supplies, clean and caulk and tallow the putrefying ships, dismiss the worst of the trouble-makers and take on instead a few more of the ordinary professional sailors of which the whole Armada was so woefully short.

Meanwhile, the commanders of the various squadrons met daily on board the *San Martin*, the Duke's flagship, putting the finishing touches to their strategy. Don Alonso was at all these meetings; he would take Don Luis as his aide, and often Miguel was allowed to go, too. In this way, he came to know all the important people very well. There were the Valdes cousins, Pedro and Diego Flores, who disliked each other intensely, despite their family ties. Don Diego was the Duke's chief-of-staff, and it was an unhappy choice, for he was a spiteful, fanatical man, whom no one liked, whereas Don Pedro, who commanded the Castilian squadron, was one of the most popular men in the fleet. Then there were the veteran sailors like Juan de Recalde, Miguel de Oquendo, and Martin de Bertendona, who had learned their craft under the great Santa Cruz. He, but for his sudden death, would have led the whole Armada—and they were determined never to let the Duke forget this fact. Miguel liked Recalde, especially—a rough, bluff, kindly man, with a sailor's red, weather-beaten face, and an openly cynical view of the whole enterprise.

It was Recalde who could be relied upon to interrupt Diego Flores' rambling, boasting speeches about Spanish invincibility and might with some casual remark about the outdated design of most of the principal Spanish galleons—or a caustic comment on the poor calibre of their guns, and the lack of trained seamen. Diego Flores would be cut off in mid-stream, suddenly deflated; one day he turned on Recalde angrily to complain: "I begin to wonder which side you are on! Don't you understand, *we cannot lose*! Why, His Majesty has actually had assurances of divine miracles working for us——"

Recalde shrugged. "And a miracle is assuredly what we shall need, if we are to catch an enemy who moves faster than we do—and avoid being blown to pieces by him! Why don't you stop prattling on so pompously, about matters you don't understand, and try putting a few of my suggestions into practice, instead?'

"How much truth do you reckon there is in Recalde's outbursts?" Miguel heard his father ask Don Alonso, at the end of a particularly quarrelsome session. "I must confess—after the past few weeks—things do not seem as simple as they once did——", a considerable admission for someone as optimistic as Don Luis had been at the beginning.

Don Alonso smiled, wryly. "I am a soldier, and the Duke is my commander. A soldier always obeys his superior officer...so I take no part in these sordid squabbles. But, as you must now know very well— and indeed, he knows it himself, that's half the tragedy! —the Duke should never have been put in charge of this affair! Not everything that has gone wrong has been his fault—the weather has been against us, and in any case the whole business has been grossly mismanaged from Madrid, from the start—but an abler leader might have been able to pull things into better shape!" He tightened his mouth. "I have no doubts about our soldiers, once we can get ashore in England, though I think the fight may be a hard one—but first of all, we have to *get* ashore! And that means wiping out the English navy. Recalde is right, for all his insubordination—our boats *are* on the slow side, and our experienced sailors are too few. We know that the English are superb on the high seas—they have proved it, time and time again. I do not believe that sheer numbers alone will crush them—only superior skill——"

"Yet, when he spoke to me, the King seemed so sure——" objected Father, still incredulous.

"The King?" Don Alonso laughed, bitterly. "The King lives in a world of fantasy, these days, Don Luis— he imagines that England is still the insignificant, bankrupt little country it was when he was there as

35

Mary Tudor's husband, thirty years ago! And these sad English refugee priests we've got aboard as interpreters encourage his delusions—it's natural, I suppose, they believe what they are desperate to believe. So they tell him that half the English are really on our side, that their ships will surrender without a fight...what nonsense! I've fought these people in Flanders. They're tough and resourceful and courageous, and they detest being dictated to by foreigners, whatever the reason. Why, even the Catholics among them will mostly choose to fight for their native, heretic Queen, rather than back a Catholic king who is a Spaniard, if they are forced to make the choice. And, speaking for myself, I cannot say I blame them—I would feel the same, in their position! Still—" he grinned, encouragingly, "I have pledged my loyalty to the King and there it is. We have had so much ill fortune so far, things must improve soon...one lucky encounter with the English fleet—a few timely hits with our big guns—and anything is possible!"

For a few days after this, Don Luis' customary ebullience was rather dampened, and he even talked vaguely of sending Miguel back to Almengo. "Perhaps your mother was right—and you *are* too young for this affair—the risks are greater than I had imagined," he admitted, ruefully. "And the issues are more complex, too—this is not the simple Crusade that I once thought it was..."

There had been several moments recently when Miguel had longed for Almengo more than anything else. During the awful bouts of seasickness, for instance, at the height of the storms; or when fever had swept the *Rata* and he had thought the stench of sweat and vomit would be with him for ever more; during the long hours of tedium, when he had been desperate to escape from the cramped conditions and the monotonous diet, and all hopes of the action and glory he had been expecting seemed doomed to disappointment. . . . But as soon as his father suggested it he slapped the idea down indignantly. To leave now would be a disgrace beyond bearing! He would never live it down! And surely, Don Alonso was right, their luck was bound to change soon. For whatever the odds against them, they had God on their side, after all . . .

So Miguel stayed. Father had been right in one respect, at least; for already he was so much more independent and self-assured, his slight limp almost unnoticeable on the rolling decks of the galleon, and his stammer quite gone. Mother would scarcely know him, when he returned home in the autumn! Indeed, as Don Luis' own self-confidence flagged, Miguel's seemed to strengthen, as if to compensate.

And, when the Armada set out again from Corunna on the last stage of its journey, some of the old St Mark's Day spirit came flooding back, and everyone felt like a conquering hero once again. At last, everything seemed to be going right. After one last, sharp storm, which had forced all four galleys to seek shelter on the French coast, even the weather turned perfect; warm and fine, with just enough breeze to help the great fleet on its way. Everyone was full of new hope and vigour. With a triumphant end to their mission surely in sight, no one was in the mood to complain or quarrel any more.

Then, early on the morning of July 30th, came the excited shout from the look-outs: "Land ahoy!"

Soon Miguel was on the bridge of the *Rata* with his father and Don Alonso, staring, wide-eyed, at the rocky Cornish coastline slipping away to their left as they sailed majestically into the English Channel, keeping their exact place in the van of the massive, crescent-shaped formation that was the Armada's pre-arranged battle-grouping. Miguel tingled with pride. It was a truly splendid sight; this great fleet, cannons at the ready, flags and sacred banners flying high, sweeping that stretch of water which the English so smugly called their very own Channel, and within sight of the English coast.... From the land, the Armada must look like a solid wall of ships, and by now the enemy must be shaking in their shoes.... But where were they? On shore, nothing stirred, and the seas were empty, too, with not even a fishing-boat in sight. It was uncanny.

"Where the devil's the enemy gone?" cried Don Alonso, half-jesting, half-impatient. "He's had plenty of notice of our arrival, after all. Such a lack of—welcome—is rather an anticlimax!" He winked at Miguel. "Perhaps we have come too early in the morning, and *el Draque* is still in bed!"

Recalde, who had been on board the *Rata* discussing tactics, gave a dry chuckle. "Do not deceive yourself! The man is not yet born, who managed to arrive too early for Francis Drake! He will not be far away, you can be sure of that!"

At that very moment, Miguel spied a movement on the cliffs. He pointed, fascinated. "*There* is our welcome!'

A thin wisp of smoke was floating upwards; as Miguel watched, it erupted into a brilliant cascade of scarlet flame and belching grey smoke. It was a warning beacon; the first of many the Spaniards were to see over the next few days, as news of the Armada's approach was flashed by bonfire from village to village, so that within no time at all the whole of England knew it was on its way.

The Spaniards were momentarily so preoccupied,

that none of them noticed one small, solitary pinnace, leaping across the waves towards them, like a cheeky young sea-horse, till it was almost beneath the *Rata's* bows....Suddenly, the decks shook, the timbers creaked and strained, as the *Rata's* cannon roared into action, and Miguel smelt, for the first time, the raw, acrid smell of gunpowder....Everyone cheered, but the shots fell wide, and the little boat danced merrily away over the horizon, the red cross of England's St George fluttering defiantly from her masthead.

"Of all the——!" Don Alonso burst into a peal of astonished laughter. "This is an enemy after my own heart," he told Father, "For it took great courage to sail that tiny boat into our midst so, even though she had the edge on us for speed....At least we can claim to be the first in the fleet to come to grips with the English—though it's a thousand pities that we couldn't score a direct hit!"

After this, Miguel fully expected the real battle to begin immediately. But instead, to his intense disappointment, a steady drizzle set in, cutting visibility to a few yards. Not another English ship came in sight, even though, by evening, the Armada was level with Plymouth, Drake's own home port.

Don Alonso grumbled tetchily, "It's unnerving, not being able to find one's enemy! I shall be much happier when we do!"

Then, as darkness was falling, four bewildered men in stained, tattered clothing were hustled aboard. They looked very frightened; and they smelt strongly of fish. One of the *Rata's* pinnaces had found them, sailing too near the Spaniards in the sea-fog. Don Alonso was delighted.

"*Some* Englishmen at last, even if they are only Cornish fishermen! At least they ought to be able to tell us where *el Draque* is hiding ... get one of those refugee priests to come and interpret ... this may be the stroke of good fortune we've been praying for!"

Three of the prisoners answered every question they were asked; they were clearly terrified out of their wits, and anxious to do anything to save their own skins. Yes, Drake had already left Plymouth, and the English fleet with him ... it would be somewhere on the open sea now, though exactly where, they had no idea ...

At this, the fourth prisoner broke into a violent torrent of abuse, reducing the other three to an ashamed silence; then, looking directly at Don Alonso, he rapped out half a dozen defiant sentences.

Don Alonso stroked his beard, smiling. "This one is a cut above the others, I fancy. What is he saying?"

"That you should not judge all Englishmen by his three compatriots ... that they are talking only to save themselves, and that you would be foolish to believe what they say ... and—" the interpreter hesitated— "That he knows full well that we have come laden with firewood and halters, ready to burn and hang every man in England, and that you can start by hanging him forthwith, because he has no intention of telling you anything at all!"

"A brave man!" applauded Don Alonso. "All the same, I believe his cowardly friends *are* telling the truth ... but I wonder where he heard this fantastic story of ropes and faggots? Part of Queen Elizabeth's campaign against us, I suppose! Tell him he's not ready for a martyr's crown yet, Master Priest. I, for one, have not come here to harm innocent people."

But as the priest began to speak again, the man rounded upon him, with a brusque sentence whose meaning—even though Miguel understood no English —was only too clear:

"Are *you* English, then?"

Silence. The priest's face flooded crimson; he dropped his eyes to the floor, said nothing, simply nodded, dumbly.

Until now, Miguel had not really bothered to consider what these English priests with the Armada stood for; he knew, of course, that they were men who had renounced their own country on account of their religion—and for him, like Don Alonso, this was something he could not fully comprehend. Spaniards were so intensely patriotic that even desertion for what they agreed to be the best of all reasons stuck in their throats!

All the same, he had an instinctive feeling for the painfully obvious dilemma of this particular individual, torn between the land of his birth and his faith. So now he watched, not really surprised by what happened, but at the same time, filled with a slightly ashamed sympathy, as, with a rattle of chains, the prisoner lurched forward, bellowing with rage.

"Traitor!" he roared—and the meaning of this was crystal-clear, too!—and he spat, hard and viciously, into the priest's face.

It was all over in seconds; two soldiers pulled the fisherman away, and began cuffing him mercilessly, only to be stopped sharply by Don Alonso, who clearly shared none of Miguel's sensibilities on the subject.

"Let him be!"

And he glanced contemptuously at the priest, who was stumbling from the cabin, wiping the spittle from his cheeks. "Had I been in this Englishman's shoes I hope I would have acted as he did," he said quietly, and gave orders for all four fishermen to be freed. "Set them adrift in their boat—they can help us no more, and this one fellow's patriotism has saved all their

41

lives, so far as I am concerned! Give me one of him for a hundred of these turn-coat priests, any day—I have no stomach for men who betray their country, whatever their reasons—even though I do happen to find them very useful!''

CHAPTER FOUR

The Road to Nowhere

In the pink, crisp glow of early dawn, the Spaniards saw that the three Falmouth fishermen had indeed been telling the truth. For there, not two miles away, lay the English fleet—but *behind* them, to the west, and not, as everyone had anticipated, approaching from the east.

Don Alonso swore softly. "It is almost unbelievable!" he exclaimed, with grudging admiration. "They must have slipped out of Plymouth in yesterday's mist, stood out to sea while we sailed by, then moved in astern of us...what superb seamanship! But it makes things exceedingly awkward!"

Miguel watched, spell-bound. Around him on the *Rata* all the last-minute battle-preparations were in full swing; officers strode back and forth, shouting orders, the gunners were priming the cannon, here and there a black-robed friar flitted in and out of the rows of assembled soldiers, murmuring words and prayers of encouragement. Was the same hustle and bustle going on among that seemingly silent forest of masts and sails, over there? he wondered. And what were the men on *those* ships saying and thinking at this moment? They were just ordinary men, like the Spaniards, after all; he knew that, now, after seeing the four fishermen yesterday...and, somehow, having seen your enemy, it was harder to hate him....

Aloud, he asked, "Does it matter that they are behind us? Can we not anchor here and fight, just the same?"

Father looked down at him, grimly unfamiliar in his battle-helmet and breast-plate. "Indeed we can—and that is what we are about to do—but since the prevailing wind is coming from the west, the English hold the weather-gauge! This means they can push us in front of them, up the Channel——"

"——Like a flock of silly sheep!" interrupted Don Alonso caustically. "Oh, we shall fight—and fight well—but the time will be of *their* choosing, not ours, and rear-guard actions are never the most inspiring. . . . And if the wind stays in the west, the English could control events right up to the time we link up with Parma! . . . ah, well! We can lead them a merry dance, even if they *are* playing the tune—and meantime, pray for a change of wind! At least we can *see* our enemy, at last!"

Now the Spaniards halted, and defied the enemy to strike; from the masthead of the *San Martin*, the standard that had been consecrated so solemnly in Lisbon flew like a sacred challenge.

Then, like a file of marauding swans, the English ships swung down the wind, heading straight for the *Rata's* stern. Oh, but they were graceful! Even the largest cut through the water as nimbly as vessels half their size. With a cry of pleasure, Don Alonso pointed to the leading ship. "The *Ark Royal*! Lord Admiral Howard's own flagship! Quickly—let's meet her broadside on as she passes—close the range—then we can grapple and board her——"

Ponderously and carefully, the *Rata* began to turn; behind her, Bertendona's *Ragazona*, the biggest ship in the whole Armada, followed suit. But they were much too slow. The *Ark Royal* was easily able to keep her distance, and her guns began firing almost nonchalantly at the *Rata*; the *Rata's* great cannon thundered in reply, and within minutes the clouds of gunsmoke were hanging over the decks like a thick, evil-smelling fog and the *Ark Royal* was completely hidden.

It was all over by midday; the English had broken off the fight and dropped back.

"If only we could have got closer!" sighed Don Alonso. "As it is, you could say we used up a great deal of shot for nothing. But at least it is a beginning. Battle has been joined at last—and not a man of ours hurt!"

Father and Miguel were lunching in Don Alonso's cabin. Everything was as formal as a Madrid banquet; even though the food was getting meagre and tasteless after so many days at sea, the salt meat and ship's biscuit was served in fine style on sumptuous gold and silver dishes by a bevy of servants, and Don Alonso had opened wine from his own personal store to celebrate the first real fighting of the campaign. It was hard to believe that they had been in the middle of a battle an hour before—almost as hard to realize that they were on board ship at all!

Don Alonso raised his glass. "Let us drink to our dining in London this day week—or fortnight at least!" he said merrily; then shook his head, and looked deadly serious. "I hope I am not tempting fate! For we still have a long way to go. Unless we can force the English to a pitched battle, and win it decisively, we are powerless to invade them—in other words, unless we can manage to wipe them off the seas very soon, this progress of ours up the Channel will have been nothing better than a road to nowhere...."

And, indeed, it was beginning to look as though the Spaniards' luck had run out on them yet again. Later that day the *San Salvador*, which was carrying most of the Armada's treasure and money, suddenly blew up, with tremendous loss of life—and rumours swept the fleet that one of the foreigners aboard must be a secret English agent who had caused the explosion deliberately. After that the unfortunate refugee priests, already unpopular enough with most of the Spaniards, became more unpopular than ever. Then Pedro de Valdes's *Rosario* was involved in a collision, and drifted out of control, straight into the arms of the English navy! The Duke of Medina Sidonia forbade his subordinates to go to Valdes's help, declaring his situation hopeless; and Valdes refused to abandon his men —and so was eventually forced to surrender to Francis Drake himself without ever firing a single shot!

"Our best gunnery commander!" bewailed Father. "Recalde and Oquendo and Don Alonso swear that Diego Flores gave the Duke that advice to abandon Don Pedro out of sheer spite ... you know how jealous he always was of his cousin's popularity ... Oquendo swears he won't speak to Diego Flores again for the rest of the campaign—and I confess, I feel much the same!"

It seemed to Miguel that things were never quite the same after the loss of the *Rosario*. When his father and Don Alonso spoke of the Duke now it was with a bitterness that had not been there before, though they were still careful not to equal Recalde and Oquendo's outspoken criticisms; nevertheless, the dissatisfaction of the leaders percolated through the rest of the ship, so that everyone became increasingly moody and irritable.

And yet, on the face of it, things were not going so badly. The Armada continued its majestic progress up the Channel, still in perfect formation, towards its rendezvous with Parma's army. Within the week, it was nearing Calais. Here the Channel was at its narrowest; from the *Rata's* bridge Miguel could see the white cliffs of Dover, floating tantalizingly on the

46

horizon in the clear light of the August afternoon sun, a mere seventeen miles away. He could see, too, the slim mastheads of the English fleet, still hot on their trail, pursuing a course exactly parallel to theirs, but a little further out to sea, just out of gunshot range.

He frowned. Only thirty miles ahead was Dunkirk, where the Spanish barges were being made ready for the English invasion. But that could not begin until the Armada had eliminated these same teasing, tormenting English ships that had been harrying it for the past eight days—these ships that were impossible to catch and grapple, impossible to pin down with shot, impossible, in the last resort, to shake off...and whose numbers seemed to grow with every day that passed, as they were joined by more and more eager volunteers from every port along the entire Channel coast...

Just outside Calais, the entire Armada suddenly changed tactics and dropped anchor—hoping against hope that the pursuing English would be taken by surprise and drift helplessly past—so leaving the Spaniards with the weather-gauge at last in their favour, perfectly poised for the final kill. But the English, as always, anticipated them. For *they* anchored too, with equal swiftness—still just out of range, but only just, and still in their dominant strategic position. All night long the two fleets faced each other, wondering what the other's next move was going to be.

For a while, when morning came, the Spaniards could scarcely believe their good fortune. The weather had not broken; there had been no English attack so far, and, indeed, while their formation held, they knew they were reasonably safe. Today, surely, much-needed reinforcements of stores and shot would arrive from the Duke of Parma, and then, weather-gauge or not, the battle, the final and decisive battle, could begin....

Then came the worst blow yet. News came trickling through that Parma's invasion force would not be ready for at least a week, and in any case, it was at present hemmed inside Dunkirk by the Dutch; and no fresh supplies could be got through from Flanders, either, because these same Dutch rebels were effectively blockading the entire Flanders coastline.

So the Armada was quite alone. It had sailed almost through the Channel—to no avail—and, in the sailing, it had virtually exhausted all its food and ammunition. With a shudder Miguel remembered Don Alonso's warning about "the road to nowhere". It looked as if they were fast approaching the end of it. And, off the shore, the wind was rising.

CHAPTER FIVE

The Final Battle

All that Sunday, the Armada lay at anchor off Calais, waiting for an attack that never came, and trying to plan for a future that was going increasingly awry.

It was unnerving, this waiting, caught like rats in a trap, with the English pressing at one's back, and only the Dutch rebels and the North Sea to flee to ahead.... From the highest to the lowest, spirits sank to their lowest ebb yet.

As dusk fell, the north-west wind freshened still further; the great ships tugged and strained at their anchors. The white cliffs of Dover had disappeared behind a cold, dull haze.

"And to think—we so nearly succeeded!" Don Luis heaved a long, sad sigh. "Those English cliffs seemed so near—almost within our grasp—but it was all an illusion! May God forgive me," he went on, bitterly, "but I have spent this whole summer chasing an illusion, even after I knew in my heart of hearts that it had no substance! I have a great deal to answer for, Miguel—to you, and especially, to your mother...she once called this whole venture a 'piece of spring madness', did she not? How right she was!"

Miguel did not know how to answer, then, for he had never known his father speak so hopelessly before, the words frightened him almost as much as the sight of those English mast-heads over there....

Don Luis twisted the little gold ring round and round

49

on his finger agitatedly—the lovers' ring that Doña Inez had given him at their parting. Miguel could see the tears standing in his father's eyes. "I had everything in the world I could have wanted," murmured Father, softly, almost as though Miguel were not there, beside him—"And yet I threw it all away—even her!—in pursuit of a dream that would be childish nonsense if it were not so stupidly tragic! It has taken me all this time to realize my folly, though, God knows, I've had warnings enough. Why, back in Lisbon, when we first saw the Duke, I ought to have seen something was very wrong . . . but I was blinded by my own imagination—I saw only what I wanted to see—just like the King! And now—it is too late!"

Miguel stared down at the waves breaking against the *Rata's* sides. They had been getting higher all day, and now, with the setting of the sun, the sea was turning an inky-black, and clawing, greedily, at the timbers. . . . A cold sweat was breaking out all over him. He was desperately afraid, yet he knew he must not show it. Above all, not now. If his nerve broke at this particular moment, he sensed that his father's would, too. "But we shall fight, all the same, shall we not?" he said, the hint of a stammer coming back for the first time in weeks, as soon as he could trust his voice not to give all his fears away.

"Oh, yes—we shall fight; but, merciful Heaven! this was not the way I intended you to gain your manhood, Miguel!" Father's voice broke. "You—who had your whole life in front of you—how can I ever expect you to forgive me?" He looked down at Miguel's strained, anxious face, and seemed suddenly to try to recapture some of his old spirit. He patted his son's shoulder. "But at least we shall show these English that we do not give in easily. . . ." And then he smiled, unexpectedly, his old self again for a moment, and, at that, Miguel felt a great load slip from him. *With Father, after all, things could never really be completely hopeless....*

That night, no one slept. Father remained on deck with Don Alonso, and Miguel begged to be allowed to stay with them. Now, huddled in his thickest cloak, he shivered miserably in the biting north-wester, privately wishing he had gone below after all.

Then—just past midnight—when the tide was running at its strongest—it happened. A small, golden blob suddenly appeared from the direction in which the English fleet had last been seen—tiny, at first, hardly more than a glimmer in the darkness, and making Miguel think, wistfully, of the fireflies that used to flit through the soft, warm Andalusian nights at Almengo. But this was no firefly. It grew steadily larger, glowing now more red than gold, and behind it, were more blobs... Then, almost imperceptibly, a sharp, hissing sound rose above the monotonous whine of the wind and the waves; and, carried along the breeze, there came the bitter taste and smell of burning...

"Mother of God! *Devil-ships!* They're trying to blow us clean out of the water!" Miguel had never before heard the beginnings of panic in Don Alonso's voice. "Weigh anchor—turn into the down-wind! Only, make haste! They're heading straight for us!"

For the first time in his life, Miguel saw men utterly transformed, almost to beasts, by blind, overwhelming fear—for what they were facing now was something quite new to them—something inhuman, faceless, unpredictable—something much more frightening than a storm or a battle against other men like themselves. And so they dashed hither and thither, wildly and aimlessly, trampling one another down. Not content with hauling up the main anchor, some hacked furiously away with their swords and cutlasses to slash clean through the cables that held the lesser ones, so that they tumbled to the seabed and were lost forever.

The ships grew closer, raining a hail of sparks, and intermittently belching gunpowder. Suddenly, instinctively, the entire Armada broke ranks and fled—east towards the treacherous shallows and sandbanks of Dunkirk and Gravelines—anywhere, anyhow, so long as it could get away from the terrifying, flaming hulks that were bearing relentlessly down upon it! For at last, the enemy had succeeded in shattering the tight defensive formation that had kept the Spaniards impregnable for so long, despite all their setbacks; and not only that. He had dealt a single, devastating blow at the long-cherished Spanish virtues of discipline and self-sacrificial courage. Whatever happened afterwards would never quite be able to wipe out the terrible memory of this one horrifying, humiliating night.

Not that the panic lasted long. The ships—empty, pitch-soaked hulks that had been set to drift shorewards with their guns primed to go off—in fact sailed harmlessly by, to burn themselves out next morning on the Calais beaches.

On the *Rata*, the shouting and the commotion slowly subsided. People began going back to their ordinary tasks, shamefaced, their voices now a little too hearty, their laughter artificially forced, in an attempt to make normality return more quickly.

"That was quite the worst error of my life!" Shaken and pale, Don Alonso reproached himself mercilessly. "I was so sure that those boats were "devil-ships" like the ones the Dutch used against us at Antwerp, three years back—filled with explosives—boats that killed and mutilated hundreds at a touch! It never crossed my mind that they were just ordinary fireships! I confess—I was scared out of my wits. It was a clever trick!" He smiled, bitterly. "A remarkably clever trick—to panic us from a reasonably safe mooring, and send us scurrying all anyhow towards the shallows and the Dutch—and we fell for it, every one of us!"

Dawn found the Spaniards still strung out in a disordered line between Dunkirk and Gravelines, drifting nearer and nearer the coastal shallows in a strong north-wester, and, with half their anchors gone, practically powerless to prevent an eventual grounding. Already the galleass *San Lorenzo* had run on to the Calais sandbanks, and Lord Admiral Howard had turned aside to batter her to pieces.

Now, at long last, the real battle began, with *el Draque* himself leading the English attack. And in the violent hours that followed, Miguel lost all sense of time, as he helped the surgeons tend the wounded, the friars to comfort the dying, against a background blurred by gunsmoke and streaked with blood.... And the noise! Long afterwards—when he was an old man, even—he would suddenly shudder with a vivid recollection of that pulverizing, agonizing noise of battle—the thunder of the cannon, the high-pitched shouting; above all, the screams of the wounded, and the hopeless muttering of those very near to death.... And, always, the grim, greedy pounding of the waves that were waiting to swallow any ship that became too waterlogged to keep going, and its crew with it....

All around him, men died; some quickly, bravely; others in a twisted, sobbing tangle of slow pain. He remembered it, much later, with tears; and wondered, at the terrible waste of it; but at the time, he scarcely felt anything at all. Certainly he never for one moment considered that he himself might end up likewise—the raw, pulped victim of the next cannon-ball, or the one after the next. In a curious sense, he felt detached from what was going on; there was none of that grasping, sickening fear of the previous night, when the fireships had struck.

Once, a veteran seaman jabbed him in the back, his voice cracked with terror: "There! Over there! That's Francis Drake!" And Miguel stared through the gun-smoke at the trim, viciously elegant *Revenge* hurtling past them, and saw, straddled on its poop-deck, a thick-set, red-bearded, slightly balding man, bawling incomprehensible orders. He crossed himself hastily, as a safe-guard lest he had just passed within musket-shot of the Devil himself!

In the hour of crisis, most of the Spaniards rallied magnificently, with all the squadron commanders recovering to come to the aid of the hard-pressed Duke and his flagship. All day long, the English pounded away at the *San Martin*; she was holed in several places, and half her men killed, but she stood her ground. Indecisive though he might be as a leader, the Duke of Medina Sidonia was no coward. And, around him, the men who had so despised him in the past— Recalde and Oquendo, Bertendona and Don Alonso —fought like tigers, indifferent to the damage their own ships were suffering, regardless of the casualties.

For a moment the English paused, astounded that such stricken, half-manned vessels could yet fight on so manfully. Then they rammed home the attack even harder. Gradually, the Spanish guns stuttered, then fell silent, as their shot was finally exhausted—and the enemy pressed on, relentlessly closing the range, pouring in fire on an enemy who could no longer return it.

It grew dark. Then, unexpectedly, the English broke off the attack, and heaved to, just out of range, their own guns also silent at last. With the dreaded sand-banks almost upon him, the Duke of Medina Sidonia signalled his battered fleet to reform in its old, proud order and fight to the death. . . . For, surely, it was far better to die in battle against an enemy like these English, than drift on to the Flanders shallows, and be slaughtered there in cold blood by the hated, rebellious Dutch. . . .

When dawn broke, grey and lowering, on the morning of Tuesday August 9th, Miguel had been on deck for more than twenty-four hours. Red-eyed, dazed from lack of sleep, he only slowly became aware that the shooting had stopped, and the shouting had died away, leaving only the moaning of the wounded lying in rows upon the open decks, and the harsh bleat of the sea and the wind, still blowing balefully from the north-west.

Someone called him. He spun round to see his father, his face haggard and ashen beneath the bloodstains and the gunsmoke streaks, one arm hanging useless at his side.

"God has remembered us! And saved us! . . . even though He would not have us win!" Don Luis' voice was little more than a whisper. "Look!" With his uninjured arm he pointed to the banner of Our Lady Queen of Heaven, sea-faded now and riddled with shot, that still fluttered from the *Rata's* main-mast. But it fluttered now in a different direction.

For in the last few moments, the wind had veered at last to the south-west—away from the treacherous shoals and the even more treacherous Dutch Zeelanders—and the Armada, though crippled, and shorter now than at the start of the battle of some half-dozen of its finest ships and several hundred of its men, was free at last to escape into the deep open waters of the North Sea!

CHAPTER SIX

The Way Back

For the moment, no one either knew or cared what the future might hold. They were too weary, too battle-sickened, too astonished by the half-miracle that had snatched them from the jaws of certain death while denying them the victory they had fought and prayed for so hard and long.

Now at last, there was time for a few hours' precious sleep. When Miguel woke again, the *Rata* was echoing to the sounds of saws and hammers as men worked to repair the worst of the battle-damage. Suddenly, the galleon seemed strangely empty; it was hard to remember how crowded she had been, not very long ago.

"There were over four hundred of us when we left Lisbon—now there are less than three," said Don Alonso, soberly. "Yet I think we shall find things even worse on the *San Martin*."

Don Alonso and Don Luis were on their way by pinnace to the first Council of War since the battle; Miguel was with them. The flagship had certainly taken heavy punishment. A whole deck had been blown away, and, with more than half her men dead, she was even more of a ghost-ship than the *Rata*.

The Duke had been hit in the leg during the battle. Diego Flores de Valdes looked nervous and ill at ease; Bertendona, whose natural reserve had given him the nickname of "the Englishman", was even less forthcoming than usual; Recalde was racked by coughing; and Oquendo, who still refused to sit round the same table as Diego Flores, was not there at all. With Father's sword-arm shattered, Miguel reflected, Don Alonso was the only one of the leaders who had come through the previous day's events comparatively unscathed.

Now it was he who broke the sad, solemn silence. "There have been differences among us in the past," he said crisply, with a hard, cold glance at Diego Flores. "But I think it should be put on the record, my lord, that your command yesterday was of the highest . . . that the outcome was not what we had hoped, does not alter that—nor the courage shown by our men. . . ."

There was a chorus of assent. The Duke nodded absently. Miguel thought how weary he looked, his hair now almost totally grey, and his face pitted with deep hollows. He seemed about to reply, when Diego Flores broke in with much of his old venom:

"One moment, Don Alonso! We had a disturbing amount of cowardice among the lesser captains—cowardice and gross dereliction of duty—and examples must be made if the discipline of the entire fleet is not to suffer——"

"——That's a good one!" Old Recalde flung back his head and roared with mirthless laughter until doubled up by another fit of coughing. "*Dereliction of duty!*" he gasped. "Can *I* be allowed to name the first such culprit, Don Diego? Whom your cousin, Don Pedro Valdes, would no doubt name also, were he here as he should be, and not rotting in some English prison owing to someone's *gross dereliction of duty——*!"

Recalde's meaning was obvious. Don Diego went white; Bertendona gave a dry snigger. At least the incident jerked the Duke out of his melancholy stupor. He said sharply, "Come, gentlemen, we are in no state to argue! Our task, today, is to agree on our next move——"

"It seems to me," said Bertendona quietly, "that there is only one move we *can* make. We still have the English pursuing us—we have several badly-holed, undermanned ships among us—and our shot is finished. Since we are being blown northwards, anyway, we should take advantage of this to return to Spain forthwith—by sailing round the northernmost tip of Scotland, skirting Ireland, and then back into the Atlantic—so avoiding England altogether. By so doing, we shall at least live to fight another day!"

"I agree!" Don Alonso nodded emphatically. "We have to face facts. Yesterday we were outmanoeuvred and outgunned. Now we are virtually defenceless. To attempt to return to the Channel would be lunacy— we would simply be lame sitting ducks for the English to finish off at their leisure!"

The Duke was scribbling idly on the paper in front of him. He looked up, his eyes dull and lifeless. "Very well. Though I am inclined to think it might have been easier to turn back and battle to the death—this voyage round Scotland and Ireland will add at least two weeks to our return to Spain, and already we are desperately short of food and water. From now on everything must be severely rationed—and the horses must be slaughtered. We can no longer afford to feed and water them too, and they are never going to be needed, now."

Miguel felt suddenly very near tears. The thought of the horses upset him more than anything he had heard all afternoon. He thought of his own Arab mare, and of how she had trusted him, and he felt like the worst sort of murderer. For days to come, he would not be able to bear to look over the galleon's side, for fear of seeing her among the scores of carcasses that were soon floating in the Armada's wake.

But the meeting was breaking up; on deck, the commanders gossiped among themselves before setting off back to their own ships. Don Alonso turned to Recalde. "We all feel as you do about Diego Flores," he said. "All the same, I think we should let the matter rest, now. In this crisis, we must all work together, even including Don Diego!"

Recalde shivered in the stiff, cold breeze. "Oh—I'll work to help get Don Diego back to Spain," he replied, softly—"And then I hope to have the pleasure of seeing him thrown into gaol for what he did to his cousin!" He began coughing again, then added, gloomily, "Though, at this moment, I honestly wonder whether this chest of mine will see me to Bilbāo— it's a deal more aggravating than a score of the Queen of England's ships! But Oquendo and Bertendona will see justice done, even if I can't!"

From the *Rata's* pinnace Miguel looked up, to see Recalde leaning over the flagship's side, smiling and waving vigorously, but again racked with coughing. He waved back.

Not for a moment did he think he would never see Recalde again.

For both Recalde and Oquendo were to die within hours of returning to Spain: Recalde, struck down by mortal sickness; Oquendo, so the story went, dying of shame on account of Spain's crushing defeat. It would be left to the coldly calculating Bertendona to give the evidence that did, indeed, send the devious Don Diego to prison for a while. And, three years later, in 1591, that same Bertendona would force yet another English ship named the *Revenge*—captained this time by Sir Richard Grenville, not Drake—into eventual surrender; and so, at the last, at least a little Spanish honour would be satisfied.

But all these events lay far in the future. And, for the present, the future was something that no one dared contemplate any more; living from one day to the next was difficult enough.

For the next four days, the battered Armada sailed steadily northwards. All the time the English hovered on its tail. During those four days the Spaniards were able to patch their shattered vessels, slaughter their horses, and bury their dead ... but there seemed no end to it. Each day, more of the men wounded at Gravelines finally succumbed. And now, with most of the remaining food stale and rancid, and the water foul, fever was breaking out again, and killing twice as many men as the English guns had done.

Then, five days after the battle, on August 13th, the look-outs could see the English no longer. The Armada's nearest landfall was now Scotland, fifty miles to the west. Confident that his enemy would never return south, Lord Admiral Howard had abandoned the pursuit, and turned back in triumph for London.

At first, the Spaniards could not believe it; they scanned the seas, expecting to see those slim, menacing mast-heads appearing again at any moment. There followed a feeling of almost light-headed relief—now there were only the waves between themselves and Spain! In the excitement of escape, it was possible to forget, for a while, that they were crawling home, humiliated and defeated.

But as the Armada turned west through the turbulent seas between the Orkneys and Shetland Isles the wind quickened, and the waves bit deep into the shattered timbers. Ship after ship began to fall away, hoping to make the shore before it sank; none was ever heard of again. The weather turned grey and cold. Men began dying of pneumonia, adding to those who died daily of dysentery and old wounds.

No one had enough to eat or drink; on the *Rata*, the galleys were unusable, the cooks mostly dead. They existed on scraps of stale biscuit, putrid water, and wine that had long since turned to vinegar. Few possessed clothes fit for this chilly, northern climate; and those they had were being continually soaked by the heavy seas breaking over the decks and pouring through the holes left after the fighting. And after so long at sea, and all that had happened, the whole ship reeked of putrefaction and decay so strongly that even the raw north-westers could not blow away the stench.

There was worse to come. As the Armada cleared the Western Isles and sailed out into the open North Atlantic, gale-force winds from the south-west whipped the seas to a malignant fury, yet prevented the fleet making any real headway. Such conditions would have tested the soundest ships and most experienced crews; but almost every vessel the Spaniards possessed was now crippled and seriously undermanned.

And yet, now was the moment when everyone forgot their old quarrels and prejudices, forgot the barriers of class and rank, and worked together in one supreme common effort to stay afloat and alive. The sons of noblemen, Miguel among them, learned to set sails, patch timbers, sluice decks; footsoldiers who till last spring had never seen the sea at all became as agile at climbing the rigging as born sailors. Some were dragged down by wounds only half-healed, others weakened by sickness and by the scurvy which was now general and which showed in the blotches and sores on their hands and faces. All were dirty, half-starved, and numbed with cold. But they battled on, day after weary day, doggedly determined to win through, somehow, to the warmth and gentleness of a Spain that now seemed more than a world away!

"Now I see why the English were content to leave us!" exclaimed Don Alonso, as the *Rata* wallowed among giant waves that reared above her mainmast, then caught and tossed her, like a pebble, down into vast hollows of boiling surf. "They believed they could safely leave the seas to put an end to us, but—" and his mouth set in a hard, firm line, "I for one intend to show them how wrong they were! And, after all, every minute that passes brings us that one minute nearer Spain!"

Spain . . . when he was taking his turn in the chain of balers, in the half-darkness, standing sometimes waist-deep in icy, stinking water, his shoulders throbbing, his fingers raw from passing the heavy pails from hand to hand, Miguel would try to concentrate on Spain. . . . Andalusia—the midday heat, the warm, caressing nights —the scented froth of orange-blossom. . . . Almengo-Real, a gleaming white pearl on the hillside, the plaintive Arabic singing of the peasants in the olive-groves . . . his mother—who must already be mourning them for dead. . . . And then his imagination would travel back to that dizzy day in Lisbon, when he had watched the Armada standard being so solemnly dedicated in the cathedral, and the bells had pealed, the cannon had thundered, the choirs had sung, and he had fancied Heaven almost joined with earth, and had believed implicitly that, with God on her side, Spain could never fear or want for anything . . . Alas! How differently things had turned out!

A hand touched his shoulder; the man who was to

take over in the baling line had arrived. Dripping and exhausted, he made his way thankfully on deck to try to rid his nostrils of the sickening stench of the bilge-hole.

The sky was lifting at long last; the wind had veered to the north-east, bringing with it the sharpness of the coming winter; it was already mid-September. There was not another ship in sight; the *Rata* was now quite alone.

But there was land—land, not five miles away—a greenish-brown haze that beckoned invitingly, that seemed to Miguel suddenly the most delectable place on earth! He licked his parched, cracked lips, thought of steady ground beneath his feet again, and fresh water in abundance...and sighed.

Don Alonso seemed to read his thoughts. He smiled slightly. "That's Ireland—and I'm sorely tempted to try and land there, even though the Duke expressly ordered us not to do so, because the Irish coast is such a dangerous one. But a few days in harbour would give us a chance to stop up the worst of our holes, and take on fresh water. After all—we've plenty of gold aboard —we could buy food from the local people, I daresay —they are Catholics like us, and they hate the English more than we do, so I've been told——"

Father shook his head. He looked old and ill; these days, Miguel reflected, he seemed to have lost all his old fire. Positive decisions no longer came naturally to him. Only when talking of Doña Inez—as he so often did, now—did he show anything of his former spirit. "But have you not forgotten the English army in Ireland?" he asked, doubtfully. "By now, news of our defeat—and of our route back to Spain—must have reached it...surely the English garrisons will have orders to attack us? After all," he went on,

64

thoughtfully, "we helped the Irish raise a rebellion only a few years back, did we not? And though it failed, I do not suppose the English have forgotten or forgiven us our part in it!"

There was a sudden gust, a swell on the water. The *Rata* quivered like a wounded animal; there was a terrifying crack of splintered wood as the mainmast split clean in two. In the stunned silence that followed, Don Alonso declared philosophically, "That settles the matter! We cannot possibly go on until we've carried out repairs! For once, I am certain we are justified in countermanding the Duke's orders—and I'll take my chance on no English army being within miles of this empty coast." He called the pilot. "Take the ship into the bay ahead—there's a purse of gold *reales* if you get us in unscathed! For the present—we stay here!"

CHAPTER SEVEN

Ireland!

The dinghy grounded in the soft shingle. Balancing his belongings on his back, Miguel leapt out excitedly, splashing towards the line of dry sand, eager to feel the solid earth beneath his feet once more. After the long weeks at sea, the ground seemed to rise up to meet him, so that at first he almost lost his balance; gritting his teeth, he stumbled on towards the grey ruin on the rise behind the sand-dunes.

Here the Spaniards were to make camp. It was not far from the shore, but to men so weakened by disease and near-starvation it seemed miles. By the time he reached the ruin, Miguel was bathed in sweat and feeling dizzy again. But he was soon off back to the beach to haul up another load. Everything of value had to be taken off the *Rata* before nightfall.

After all the terrible violence of the past weeks, the battles and the tempests, they seemed to have arrived at the most peaceful place in the world. There was not a cottage, not a boat in sight, and no sound, except the waves scraping the shingle, the screaming gulls overhead, and their own voices. Certainly there was no trace of any English, nor even of the wild Irish whom some of the sailors had heard of, and who were said to live off the treasure they salvaged from wrecks, and not to be over-particular about what happened to the survivors! No one noticed a few shadowy figures, crouching in the marram grass, slip silently away into the gloom behind the ruined fortress.

Still, it was best to be sure. Don Alonso mounted a guard on all sides, with strict orders to report anything unusual. A few men, led by the Italian pilot who had brought them safely into the bay, begged to move on at once; but this Don Alonso rejected out of hand.

"Tonight we stay here," he declared. "We have the sea at our backs, and the *Rata* within easy reach, dismasted though she is. No one knows what lies inland. Morning will be time enough to find out."

Even the guards soon drifted into an exhausted sleep. So no one noticed the pilot and his friends pick their way over the other sleepers and slip from the castle, quite determined, despite Don Alonso's orders, to go their separate way.

The moon rose, turning bay and shore and castle to silver, and shining directly on the guard posted to survey the beach. He woke with a guilty start, and what he saw made him rush to waken Don Alonso. Soon everyone was on his feet, staring in amazement at the strange sight on the sands below. It was as if they were all dreaming the same bad dream! For twenty or thirty men, women and children were rowing back and forth in little coracles between the shore and the *Rata* and swarming all over her decks. They were fast stripping her of everything that was still on board—chests and hangings, cushions and platters not valuable enough to bring ashore—and some of them were even prising up planks and ripping the panelling from the cabins.

"We shall soon have no ship left, if this continues!" exploded Don Alonso, caught between amusement and anger; and, striding boldly down to the shore, he signalled his men to follow him.

The people on the beach took not a scrap of notice, but went calmly on with what they were doing. And in the middle of the sands, two girls danced a furious, whirling dance, dressed, so far as Miguel could tell, in the tapestries he had last seen around the bed in Don Alonso's own cabin!

One young captain drew his sword. "There's only one way to stop this!" But as he did so, a couple of the men detached themselves from the rest, and circled him menacingly, waving long, ugly knives.

"Put your sword away! We need these people as friends——" cried Don Alonso; then he stopped, as he saw a tall, gaunt figure walking over the shingle towards him.

The man halted, and bowed—a deep, gracious bow—and began speaking in a strange, flowing language quite unlike anything Miguel had ever heard before. He was very tall—almost as tall as Don Alonso—and very old, with long, white hair and a flowing beard, and was shrouded in a great, black cloak. The rest of the Irish stopped what they were doing, and clustered behind him, silent; even the girls stopped their dancing.

Don Alonso bowed in return. "We come as friends," he said. "We were part of the King of Spain's army—that was to have invaded England, who is your enemy as much as ours. But we failed; and now we ask you to help us to return to Spain."

The old man shook his head. It was clear that he had not understood. The Spaniards were equally at a loss—for none of them knew a word of the Irishman's Gaelic.

Then one of the refugee interpreter priests pushed his way to the front. "Some of them speak English, my lord, though they do not like to do so...let me try...."

The effect of the Englishman's voice was devastating. First a deathly hush, then a noisy hissing and spitting. One of the men with the knives walked slowly towards the speaker, balancing his weapon threateningly in the palm of his hand.

The old man glared. Miguel noticed that his eyes were a strange, fiery blue. Then, pushing the man with the knife contemptuously to one side he also spoke in English—just a few sharp words. And the priest answered equally shortly, presumably explaining his own reasons for being an Englishman on the Spanish side. And this time the reaction was very different—and very different, too, from that of the Falmouth fisherman, all those weeks back!

Holding out his hands, the old man began to speak, passionately, having at one point to brush the tears from his eyes. And, all the while, Spanish and Irish alike stood by, desperate to know what was going on.

At last came a pause. The priest turned to Don Alonso. "This man is a bard—a wandering poet and minstrel. His name is Sean. In Ireland such men are greatly respected, because their songs teach the glories of ancient Ireland. Sean says he sang in the great halls of the Irish chieftains in his youth, and even in the lords' houses in Dublin, which is where he learned his English. But now the halls of the chiefs are destroyed, and there is a price on his head, for the English have forbidden the bards to sing any more . . . so that not a word of English has passed his lips for forty years, until today."

These poor Irish peasants, Sean explained, lived by scratching a living from the scrub near the sea, and so welcomed a shipwreck to provide them with a little extra. They had little enough to eat themselves, but all they had, they were ready to share with the Spaniards. In return, however, they must be allowed their pick of the *Rata's* possessions, since that had been the custom regarding wrecks in Ireland since the beginning of time,

70

and one that not even the English had been able to change...

"They are welcome to what is on board," replied Don Alonso frankly. "And we will pay in gold for what we take from them. But if they go on hacking the *Rata* to pieces as they are doing at present, there will soon be nothing left of her!"

Sean shrugged his shoulders, curling his lip scornfully. Any fool could see that the *Rata* was past repairing; she would never sail again—so let his people have her— she was theirs by ancient right, after all! Don Alonso was still reeling under the calm assurance of this astonishing statement, when Sean went on to declare that, in any case, there was another Spanish ship in the next bay—and one that was still seaworthy. At dawn, he would send out his messengers; this second vessel could be in Blacksod Bay before the next moonrise, and Don Alonso and his company could then continue their journey aboard *her*...

Another Spanish ship! How was this possible? But as Don Alonso hesitated, frowning in unbelief, yet knowing that he was in fact powerless to prevent these Irish doing exactly as they pleased, Sean continued:

"You should not stay here a moment longer than necessary! For the present, you are safe; my people will never betray you. But there is an English garrison not thirty miles away, and news travels fast. Already, a dozen of your men have set off inland. That was a foolish thing to do. If they fall into English hands they will very soon be forced to give your hiding-place away."

On learning of the disappearance of the Italian pilot and his cronies, Don Alonso flew into a fury. "We are all lost if we do not stay together now! I swear I will personally hang the next man who tries to desert!"

There were not many English soldiers in Ireland, altogether, went on Sean, "And yet those there are, are everywhere. And here in Connaught it is the worst of all, because Sir Richard Bingham, the Governor, is the most ruthless of all the English Governors—more so, even, than the Lord Deputy, who is supposed to be his superior!" And Sean rocked to and fro in his grief as he described how, already, other ships from the Armada had been forced to land in Ireland—some driven ashore by starvation, others violently ship-wrecked. The English had shown little mercy to any of them; but the Governor of Connaught and his brother had shown least of all. In Galway, they had publicly executed more than three hundred Spaniards who had sur-rendered to them. "There was nothing we could do," mourned Sean, "save make shrouds for the dead and pray for their souls. So long as the English do not know you are here," he added, "we will help you all we can. But once you are discovered—we are powerless. We are a conquered nation," he concluded, bitterly, "with few possessions left to us, and even fewer rights! Be thankful that, though you may have been defeated, you still have a country to return to! For ours does not belong to us any more!"

But next morning, it was hard for the Spaniards to believe that they had indeed not all dreamt the previous night's events. For the bay was as empty as it had been on their landing. The sea had washed away all traces of the evening's visitors. Worse still, on the rising tide the *Rata's* only remaining anchor had broken loose, and she was solidly grounded in the shingle. She was now obviously a total wreck.

There was a general air of depression that even Don Alonso found difficult to dispel. They had struggled so hard, and suffered so much—but for what? Spain was still hundreds of miles away. And, who could tell? Maybe some of the luckier vessels in the Armada were already back there—while they rotted here in Ireland, quite forgotten...

And then, this fanciful talk of a second ship! Moonshine, surely—and how could anyone as normally level-headed as Don Alonso have believed such foolish talk from a rambling old madman? There were murmurings among the more disgruntled—a few whispers, even, of marching off to surrender to the English—for Sean's talk of their cruelty was surely just another Irish exaggeration!—and even the return of the Irish, laden with food, and with Sean riding at their head on a little black donkey, failed to revive their flagging spirits.

Yet it should have done, as everyone knew in his heart. For the Irish, poor though they were—and in the morning sunshine Miguel could see that they were poorer by far than any Spanish peasants he had ever seen, and actually more gaunt than the half-starved Spaniards they were now helping—had brought with them all the food they possessed—even to the pig that they were fattening for Christmas! They rejected all payment, and when Don Alonso tentatively suggested that what they had brought should at least be divided between themselves and the Spaniards, Sean retorted with dignity, "Poor we may be, but we are proud, too. We were kings and princes when the rest of Europe were barbarians! What we have is freely offered—take it!"

But the meat and oatcakes and sour milk did not go far among so many. At the end of it all, the Spaniards felt themselves no better off—their ship completely useless, and this promise of a second one just so much Celtic fantasy.... As the day went by, with the Irish still placidly stripping the *Rata's* remains to the bare hulk, as if it were the most natural thing in the world, and not another boat came in sight, Don Alonso grew more and more uneasy.

"If this legendary vessel doesn't materialize soon, I shall have a mutiny on my hands!" he declared. "I was mad to be so trusting last night—we should never have landed in this accursed place, broken mast or not! Ask the bard what price his promises, now!"

On hearing this, Sean flew into a terrible rage, seeming to stand even taller and wilder than before, his eyes flashing like hot coals, and his hands stretching before him, as if in a kind of trance. Then he stopped, abruptly. The strange light died from his face. Mounting his little donkey, he rode away over the dunes, without so much as a backward glance, his people following him.

The interpreter turned a stricken face to Don Alonso. "He was claiming the second sight, my lord—and he cursed you for doubting him, and said you would live to regret it. . . . Do not be so anxious to see this second ship, he said, for it is not the one in which you will finally escape from Ireland; there is a third yet to come —and that will be the last boat in which you ever sail at all!"

There was a horrified silence; men crossed themselves and shuddered; Miguel saw his father's drawn face quiver, ever so slightly, and felt himself shaking uncontrollably. Only Don Alonso was unabashed. "It scarcely needs Celtic second sight to tell me that once finally I set foot in Spain I shall take good care never to trust myself to the sea again as long as I live!' he cried, half-joking. Then he looked rueful. "But I am sorry I made the bard angry—for he has done us much service——"

He was interrupted by one of the look-outs, shouting

hysterically. The Spaniards looked—and looked again.... *Sure enough, a second galleon was sailing into the bay!* Scarcely daring to breathe, lest the spell broke, they watched her make slowly for the opposite shore and drop anchor.

"God forgive my unbelief! The old man was right!" Don Alonso was the first to recover his voice. "Come," he went on, more prosaically, "we must march round to her at once—for fear she sets sail again without us!"

They were less than half-way there, when they saw men running to them from the other ship. Each group, seeing the other, hurried the faster; the leaders grasped each others' hands, laughing, almost weeping, with joy. For both had believed themselves quite alone on this wild coast; had begun to imagine that all their comrades were, indeed, dead; meeting others in a like plight seemed to make all their problems suddenly less serious. There was a kind of magic safety in numbers.

"We were in the Andalusian squadron," the leader of the second ship told Don Alonso. "Our damage is not serious—but we have lost a lot of men through sickness. Our captain and pilot both died last week. We were forced ashore when our water ran out; the Irish helped us, then told us about you——"

"And about the English garrison too, no doubt?" said Don Alonso. And when the young officer commanding the *Duquesa Santa Ana* nodded—"Then you realize the danger we are in while we stay here. Our discovery can only be a matter of time—and now that I've so stupidly offended Sean we can expect no further help from him.... Can you take us on your ship? There are only a hundred of us left now, to add to your two hundred——"

"Gladly!" The young man was enthusiastic. "With you to lead us, Don Alonso, how can we fail to get back to Spain safely? For the joint command must be yours, that goes without saying—I stepped in only when those above me had died."

Don Alonso grinned. "Let's hurry aboard then! I confess, I'll be greatly relieved to get back to sea— which is something I never thought I would say— there is something very threatening about this great, empty bay——"

He stopped. For Sean was returning, riding his little donkey at a tremendous gallop, his white hair streaming in the wind. Straggling behind were his peasants, shouting and waving wildly.

"We must sail at once—or face certain death!" cried the interpreter. "He says that Sir Richard Bingham has captured our pilot and his friends and hanged every one of them...but he made them tell him first, where we were....A detachment of cavalry is on its way now— we have but a few minutes' start!"

Barely was the last Spaniard aboard, when a posse of horsemen appeared on the skyline, then plunged over the dunes, galloping furiously towards the open beach. The Irish scattered and vanished among the rocks. To their warning the Spaniards certainly owed their lives.

For by now the *Duquesa Santa Ana* was edging her way cautiously towards the open sea. Everyone held his breath; the man doing the pilot's job today was a simple Bilbão fisherman, used only to navigating his three-man mackerel boat, and working without charts; if they grounded here, they were as good as dead.

But all went well. The Englishmen were left, frustrated and fuming, at the water's edge; Miguel thought he could make out Sean, still watching them, broodingly, from the shadows beneath the cliffs. Try as he might, he could not get the Irishman's prophecy out of his head; for him, it had an ominously sinister ring, and could be made to mean something very different from the interpretation placed on it so light-heartedly by Don Alonso...

He told himself not to be stupid. Don Alonso clearly had no worries—or did not show them. "Now—back to Spain!" he cried—"And as fast as possible! We have scarcely any stores aboard—so—unless we want to starve—we must sail like demons!"

But this was easier said than done! They were sailing in the teeth of a strong headwind, and when morning came, Blacksod Bay was still in sight. At this rate, the food on board could never last them even half-way back to Spain.

"It is no use—" Don Alonso conceded—"We must turn around—get the wind behind us—and head for Scotland instead! The Scots will surely help us—their Queen was executed by the English only last year, after all—and we can be in Scotland long before we starve!"

So they turned north, moving fast now—almost too fast. The sails, rotten after so long at sea, were ripped to shreds, and the boat began to ship water badly. And, as the wind drove them north, so it drove them east, too—nearer and nearer the shore, nearer and nearer the jagged rocks that ran far out to sea here, and whose full extent they could only guess.

There was a rocky inlet ahead, and now the sinking galleon headed for it desperately. There was no alternative; the Spaniards were going to have to land in Ireland once again; and pray, a second time, that no English army would be waiting for them!

At the bay's mouth, a gigantic wave picked the boat up like a tiny toy, and hurled her forward, pitching her into the bank of rocks and shingle at the water's edge. She slid down among the stones, listing heavily, her back broken. Water poured over her; men, masts and cannon were flung from one end of her sliding decks to the other.

It was a miracle that no more than a score of men drowned in this second shipwreck. The rest struggled ashore, to huddle in a cave above the waterline, waiting for the storm to subside and for dawn to break.

Don Alonso lay in their midst, both his legs broken. As the boat grounded, the capstan had broken loose and crashed down upon him; it was Don Luis, one-armed though he was, who had managed to drag him free. Everyone had come to think of Don Alonso as quite indestructible; now, his injuries deepened their despair. Without *him* to lead them—how could they possibly go on?

It was two months to the day since the Armada had sailed from Corunna with such high hopes. Now, the first battered ships were just beginning to limp back into the harbours of north-west Spain. At this very moment, the Duke of Medina Sidonia's *San Martin* was actually dropping anchor at Santander, and the unfortunate commander was soon scurrying back to his orange-groves, pursued by bitter, taunting crowds who cat-called "Here comes Drake!" whenever his coach came in sight. But the anger and the mockery rapidly turned to an overwhelming sense of despair, as the trickle of returning ships dried up, and all Spain mourned the almost certain loss of the rest. One hundred and thirty ships had left Spain in that dizzy, hopeful spring: less than half were to return, and the dead ran into tens of thousands. Hundreds of men were massacred by the English in Ireland alone, where over a score of vessels were to be shipwrecked.

The whole country was convulsed with a terrible

grief; from now onwards, Spain's ambitions withered, her horizons shrank, and the slow fall into decline began. And the two hundred and fifty men shivering in the cave in far-off Donegal had long ago been written off as dead.

CHAPTER EIGHT

The Long Walk

Now Father took over temporary command. For a little while, the sudden and unexpected responsibility seemed to shake him out of the dull lethargy into which he had fallen over the past weeks. As soon as it was light, he sent a search-party up the cliffs. "The *Duquesa Santa Ana* will never sail again," he said flatly; and then, raising his voice to drown the dubious muttering that had started up again, and speaking with such conviction that only Miguel sensed how forced his optimism really was "—But, after all—we know now that several other Spanish ships have reached Ireland ahead of us. Who knows? One of them could well be anchored not too far from here! There could still be a means of escape, if only we can find it. . . ."

It was a raw, windy day; but the storm had passed. Most people were glad to get down to work, simply to keep warm. The able-bodied were sent back to the wreck, to bring ashore everything worth salvaging; and the chests of coins and jewellery, clothes and documents were stored at the back of the cave along with the muskets and what little food remained.

Soon the search-party returned, bringing with it another group of Irish peasants—less poverty-stricken, these, than the last—together with their priest. This time there was no need of an English interpreter; for the priest could speak Latin, which was the common language of both the Church and of educated men the world over, so that Don Luis had no difficulty in understanding him, and even Miguel could follow most of what was being said.

"You are no longer in Connaught," explained the priest—and at this, there were heartfelt sighs of relief all round! Perhaps, after all, they could escape slaughter a little while longer! "This is Donegal, to the north, in the province of Ulster. Though we have an English governor here, too, he is less harsh than Bingham. Besides, in Ulster, there are still Irish chieftains with real power—like The O'Neill. Hugh O'Neill was brought up in England, and Queen Elizabeth favoured him, and made him Earl of Tyrone, believing him her man. But this English pose of his is only a cover— O'Neill hates the English still, and is only biding his time until he can lead a rising against them. Already, he has helped many of your countrymen to escape across to Scotland——"

"So we have no English garrison to fear on our doorstep?"

Everyone started in amazement at the sound of Don Alonso's voice. He had regained consciousness at last, and was lying on a makeshift stretcher at the back of the cave, his broken limbs bound in splints. Though he looked deathly pale and ill, he was as lucid and decisive as ever.

"No—although parties of soldiers are scouring all these coasts, hunting for Armada survivors—but this is a very isolated place—none have penetrated here, so far. They must first pass through O'Neill's territory, and that he can mostly prevent——"

"But not indefinitely, I imagine," mused Don Alonso. "Somehow, we must get to Scotland before we are discovered ... the English are not fools, and two hundred Spaniards are not easily hidden ...

"If only there—was another ship!"

"Ah!" The priest sighed, regretfully. "In fact, there are *three* Spanish vessels on the far side of this peninsula, in Donegal Bay, carrying nearly five hundred men between them—but two are total wrecks—and the survivors of the third have all but mutinied, and refuse to do anything to make their ship sea-worthy again.... McSweeny Banagh, the chieftain whose land they are on, and who took them in when they were wrecked, is near to handing them all over to the English as the only way of getting them off his hands before they eat everything he has! In any case—" he looked doubtfully at the ragged, emaciated men in front of him— "All these ships are fifteen miles away—and it's a hard march, at the best of times——"

His objections were drowned by Don Alonso's roar of delight. "There you are! Sean the bard was right! My third ship!" He grinned; but Miguel felt suddenly sick and afraid at the mention again of those cryptic words; and he wondered how many others felt as he did. But Don Alonso was plunging merrily on. "If but one of these three ships can be made seaworthy again, it's enough!" He raised himself shakily on one elbow. "Five hundred men—and our own two—granted, that's a heavy load for one vessel—but she only has to get us as far as Scotland.... Do you know anything more about this third ship, Master Priest?"

"—Only that she is one of the Naples galleasses—and called the *Girona*."

"Better and better!" Don Alonso beamed. "Those galleasses are big boats—after all, they have to carry three hundred rowers, as well as an ordinary ship's complement—and they are steady, even though they are slow—so there should be no more shipwrecks!" He looked grave. "As for all this talk of a near-mutiny....

I'll soon put an end to that!"

Once more, everyone was swept forward on Don Alonso's irrepressible enthusiasm. With him to lead, anything was possible. And later that day, when the Spaniards started out for Killybegs, with the Irish priest to guide them, Don Alonso led them as he always had, even though this time he had to travel in a litter hammered together with timbers taken from the wrecked galleon. Relays of men took turns to carry him but progress was slow and erratic. No one had strength enough left to walk very fast; many were weak from hunger, sickness, or old wounds, and before long many more were limping from new sores acquired on the march itself. For the road was a hard one, as the priest had warned them—first through bog and scrub, then climbing among rocky outcrops; and by now most people were barefoot, and reduced to tearing strips from their already tattered clothes to wrap around their bruised, bleeding feet.

It took three days to cover those fifteen miles. On the first, it rained continually, and then a choking mist swept in from the sea, chilling everyone to the marrow. After that, the days turned hot and sultry again, though the nights were bitterly cold and damp. As they dropped to marshier ground on the southern side of the peninsula, swarms of gnats and midges emerged to harass them. They drank water from the streams, ate berries, grass, even roots plucked from the wayside. But they were always hungry. Though the local peasants gave them food, they had little enough to offer. Sometimes only Don Alonso's iron discipline prevented his men from fighting among themselves to the death over the ownership of a handful of oatcakes. They had set out singing—the songs of Catalonia and Castile, of Aragon and Andalusia—defiantly determined to keep up their spirits. By the last day, even talking was an effort too hard to make. Every ounce of energy was needed simply to keep going. For some, even that too was too much; the road from Loughros More Bay to Killybegs was lined with the rough wooden crosses of men who had died on the journey.

All through the nightmare weeks in the Atlantic, Miguel had been able to close his mind to the grim realities of the present, and travel back in his imagination to Almengo-Real, or Seville, or Lisbon—to the places and people of his happiest moments. But now he found he could no longer play such tricks with his memory; his mind obstinately refused to budge from the miseries of the present. His body ached and itched; he was either sweating under a humid sun or shivering through the bitter nights. On the second day his boots finally fell to pieces, and after that every step was a kind of minor torture.

Yet Miguel's plight was not nearly so bad as most. The past weeks' experiences had left him taut and wiry, stronger and more self-reliant than he had ever dreamed he could be; whereas his father's battle-wound had led to a fever that had turned Don Luis into almost an old man, physically, and his will to survive had long since been blunted by the shattering of all his most cherished illusions. Indeed he had been a defeated man even before the Armada had been defeated; now, even the memories of his wife, of Almengo, could scarcely touch him. Time and again he would stumble and fall by the wayside, muttering that he only wished to be left to die in peace, and Miguel had often half to carry, half to drag him.

Indeed but for Don Alonso, most of the Spaniards would have given up long ago. Despite his own injuries, Don Alonso's energies were inexhaustible, and his resolve never once wavered. At each halt, he would go the rounds, urging his men to fresh efforts, declaring that no army in history had ever acted more bravely than they were doing now. "The English may have beaten us in battle, but they can never break us!" he told them. "We shall prove, once and for all, that there is no such thing as an utterly defeated Spaniard!" And so, almost miraculously, the half-starved, tattered columns staggered on.

Then, on the fourth morning, they suddenly came upon the sea glistening below them, and the great galleass they had come to find bobbing at anchor in the little harbour there. There was a ragged cheer; even the feeblest tried to walk a little faster. Miguel turned triumphantly to his father: "You see! We shall get home, after all! I know we shall!" and was rewarded by seeing Don Luis raise his hand to his lips, kissing Mother's little gold ring for the hundred-thousandth time, and smile as he had not smiled for many weeks past.

Don Alonso, of course, was already planning for the future. "We can use the materials from the other two wrecks to patch up the *Girona*," he said, enthusiastically. "Nothing is impossible, now that we are here . . . and Scotland is probably not more than a day's sail away!"

The track fell steeply into the bay; everything seemed soaked in a blue, translucent glow. The Spaniards would soon come to accept this almost ethereal brilliance as a fine day commonplace in Ireland; but now, seeing it for the first time, after their days of misery in the gloomy, lowering mountains, they felt as if they were entering Paradise itself. On the fishermen's cabins, the nets were drying in the sun; as the marchers approached, men, women and children gathered round, staring, waving, smiling.

All round Miguel, grown men were brushing the tears from their eyes. It all seemed so peaceful; it was hard to realize that they were still fugitives in a country governed by an enemy who was bent on their total destruction! The numbness melted from his mind, and he remembered nostalgically that other procession, down another hill, and how the people then had come out of their cottages to wish them well on their triumphant way to England.... Ah, if only they had known then what they knew now!

Along the shore, the five hundred survivors of the three Spanish vessels were camped in an untidy jumble of hastily-built mud cabins. And, as the priest had hinted, they were simply sitting about, doing nothing—dicing, brawling, sleeping. The whole encampment was dirty and derelict; the men in it, sullen and unkempt. In one corner about a hundred men were penned like cattle inside a rough palisade. They were the galley-slaves—all that remained of the *Girona's* original three hundred rowers.

Father followed Don Alonso's disapproving stare. "I suppose the rest thought that if the galley-slaves were allowed to go free, they would make their way straight for the English."

Don Alonso shook his head. "Not when I have spoken to them. The English make no distinctions about whom they hang in Ireland—freeborn Spaniards and Turkish galley-slaves are all one and the same to them! We need these people to help us get the *Girona* to Scotland—but they will never row unless they are better treated. Besides—" he shrugged—"Poor devils! Convicts, Turks, Moors—they did not ask to get involved in our war, after all!"

When Don Alonso made up his mind about anything, action invariably followed at once. Now, sweeping aside a few feeble protests from some of his fellow-officers, he rapidly saw to it that the galley-slaves were released from the stockade, the manacles struck from their wrists. Then he appealed for their help, speaking as man to man, passionately, persuasively, as only he could. "I give you my solemn word," he cried, "that if we succeed in getting away from here you will all be made free men when we reach Spain—regardless of why you were sent to the galleys! And I have never in my life gone back on my word, as many here can testify!" And the galley-slaves rose to him as one man, cheering, weeping, promising all he asked, leaving those who had doubted them stunned into shamed silence.

Then Don Alonso turned his attention to shaking the Spanish loungers by the shore out of their lethargy. He flattered, then bullied; cursed, then cajoled. "There are seven hundred of us here altogether now," he declared. "Surely, between us, we can get this boat shipshape enough to make the single day's voyage to Scotland? From there, our return to Spain is easy. . . ." He smiled, half-apologetically. "I fear we shall have missed the wine-harvest, but at least we'll be home before Christmas! After all we have gone through, all we have suffered—surely we can make this one last effort? Do not our loved ones, who put so much trust in us, deserve this of us? There is everything to gain if we do—and our honour, as well as our lives, to forfeit if we do not!"

CHAPTER NINE

The Third Ship

Under the spell of Don Alonso's words, the lazy, idle rabble on Killybegs beach rapidly became, once again, a disciplined, enthusiastic force. For as always, Don Alonso's personality worked like a charm. Soon, the whole encampment was transformed, acquiring a sort of military order. The only men still idle were those who were too sick or weak to work.

Work on the *Girona* went steadily ahead; it was made all the harder because few of the Spaniards were experienced shipwrights. And they lacked the ideal tools and materials. So they could only patch, and not replace the badly-damaged rudder without which the galleass was useless.

It all took time—and after a few days the dour McSweeny Banagh, on whose land the Spaniards were encamped, began to grumble again that feeding what amounted to a small army was more than he could manage, even at the considerable price in gold that Don Alonso was paying him; and that from now on the Spaniards would have to be content with horseflesh rather than the sides of beef and mutton he had been supplying at the beginning!

But by the third week in October, the *Girona* was almost shipshape. Now replacements had to be found for the two hundred galley-slaves who had died between Corunna and Ireland—for without the full three hundred rowers, the galleass would be too cumbersome to manoeuvre. Such rowing was something that even the poorest Spaniard would not normally dream of doing, and the idea of sitting cheek by jowl with a convicted murderer or heathen Turk was especially distasteful. But, once again, Don Alonso's appeal brought in all the volunteers he needed.

"Now we are almost ready!" he grinned, as he watched the rowers coming ashore after their first practice attempt, rubbing their aching shoulders and blistered palms. "In a couple of days, we should be safe in Scotland! Loading can start tomorrow at first light!"

Miguel glanced across the bay at the *Girona*, hoping that the apprehension he could not help feeling was not apparent on his face. Try as he could, he found it impossible to get Sean's strange prophecy out of his head, and, despite all his admiration for Don Alonso, he found the latter's explanation of it basically unconvincing. . . . All in vain, he told himself that he was being foolish, and letting his imagination run dangerously away with him . . .

Perhaps, he thought, he felt as he did because the last few weeks had been so much happier and more stable than for a long time past. After the hardships of the last few months, the stay in Killybegs had marked the return to a relatively placid, routine existence. The fickle weather of late summer had given way to long, clear days of autumn sunshine; the harbour waters glowed azure and tranquil, and looked incapable of producing anything more terrifying than the gentlest of ripples. Father, too, was stronger and more cheerful, talking constantly of Mother and Almengo, discussing what he would do when he got home again, planning for Miguel's future . . . but, of course, there could be no future for any of them without a voyage in this giant, somehow sinister boat, across a sea which was frightening enough in itself without Sean's cautionary words to add to its terror . . .

The *Girona* had been carrying much of the lost *San Salvador's* treasure; and all this, which had been kept on shore under guard, had now to be reloaded. Then there were all the possessions salvaged from the other two wrecks in Killybegs Bay, as well as the remaining chests and bundles from the *Rata* and the *Duquesa Santa Ana*, which had been manhandled here across the peninsula so painfully.

At the start of the venture, Miguel and his father had had baggage enough to fill an entire dinghy; what they were left with now barely covered the bottom of a single chest. And of all Don Luis' followers who had set out so hopefully with him from Lisbon in the *Rata*, none were now alive. His fighting-men had all perished during or after the Gravelines battle, and his servants had died, one by one, miserably, on the journey to Ireland and after, the last of them buried only a few weeks before on the hard road to Killybegs.

Don Luis' conscience gave him little peace, even in this peaceful bay. When he was at his most depressed and destructive he would bewail the loss of his own men in particular and put the guilt for their deaths squarely on his own shoulders.

"I dragged them into this, Miguel, I misled them with tales of glory and easy victory. But for my lunatic day-dreams they would all be alive now. If you survive me, and get back to Almengo, you must see to it, above all else, that their dependants are provided for. Promise me that!" And Miguel would nod, and promise, not once, but many times over, not wholly understanding the full tragedy of it yet, and ashamed that he did not feel more moved—but saying anything to get that haunted, lost look from Father's despairing eyes...

Now, as Miguel snapped the chest to, his own sharpest pang of regret was still for the might-have-been—the sunny landing on the English beaches, the triumphant progress into London town, the crowds cheering their liberators... but then, would they have cheered? Now that he had seen the English fight, he was not so certain any more...

There was a sudden commotion; he looked up, and froze with horror; a procession of horsemen was making straight for the Spanish camp—had the English discovered them, at last? For these new arrivals were not poor Irish peasants on donkeys and scrub-ponies! Their leader could have stepped straight from a Spanish castle —except that men with hair as flaming auburn as his were not often seen in Spain. He was handsome, thickset, his fashionably-clipped hair and beard streaked with grey. A heavy gold chain, richly encrusted with precious stones, glimmered against the dark velvet of his doublet. Miguel stared, acutely conscious of his own faded rags; he had come to assume that all the Irish, even if not poor, were ill-clad and shabby.

The horsemen halted. The red-haired man spoke— and in Spanish, too—strongly accented and halting, but Spanish for all that. "I have come—in friendship—to visit your commander, Don Alonso Martinez de Leyva," he said, smiling. "Will you take me to him? I am Hugh O'Neill, Earl of Tyrone."

So *this* was the great Irish lord who kept his lands by appearing the Englishmen's friend—and yet who, so the Donegal priest had whispered, was secretly the sworn enemy of England and all she stood for! Had he come with a warning? Or to offer help? And could he really be trusted, anyway?

From the beach, O'Neill looked reflectively at the

Spanish encampment and smiled. "My compliments, Don Alonso.... You seem to have welded your assorted company into a real army! McSweeny Banagh tells me you drill and practise every day, as if preparing for a battle, rather than a flight back to Spain—which brings me to the reason for my visit—" He paused, momentously. "I have come to ask you to stay the winter—" he waved his hand as Don Alonso opened his mouth to protest. "Oh, I would not ask you were it not absolutely safe for you to do so—far safer, in fact, than setting off for Scotland at this time of year in that great floating castle over there...." He glanced, somewhat scornfully, Miguel thought, at the *Girona*; and once again, Miguel was reminded of Sean's prophecy, and he felt a stab of panic, and, for another horrifying but mercifully brief moment, saw the *Girona*, not as a means of escape, but as an instrument of terrifyingly impending doom...

But Don Alonso was talking. "We shall sail safe enough." His reply was crisply short. "Ireland is no place for Spaniards to linger, these days....We have heard what happened in Galway——"

"——Ah, but that was in Connaught—Bingham's province! Ulster is quite different!" O'Neill smiled, reassuringly. "We Irish still count for something in Ulster—and besides, the English have—it can only be accidentally!—given us a governor who is a gentleman ...and so all the easier for me to take advantage of! And, I confess, I am not asking you to stay primarily on account of your own comfort—though you could certainly take shelter in one of my castles for the winter...." He laughed suddenly, showing a row of white, gleaming teeth, but his eyes were cold, green-grey, like a predatory fox. When he spoke again he was deadly serious. "Through the winter we could both

93

gather fresh supplies—you could send to Spain, while I assembled my own forces, and found new allies ... then, come spring, we would be ready to start a rebellion together, that would sweep the English out of Ireland forever, and weaken Elizabeth beyond your king's wildest dreams!" O'Neill looked reproachful. "King Philip should have had the Armada sail direct to Ireland—you would have found a whole nation waiting to welcome you! Still, with *you* here, Don Alonso, it is not too late, even now, to turn a terrible defeat into a glorious victory—for both our countries! Will you help me?"

Don Alonso shook his head. "I have no proper army here," he said, wearily, "Simply a few hundred tired, dispirited men, anxious only to see Spain again.... They have neither the will nor the strength for a battle. I have kept them drilling merely to preserve their discipline. However—" he smiled, faintly—"When I reach Madrid, I will tell King Philip what you have said. No doubt he will want to send you all the help he can, but—" he shrugged—"I must tell you candidly, my lord, for I fear Madrid never will, that after such a defeat as we have suffered this year, that help may not in fact be very much." He sighed. "I admire your spirit. In happier times, you and I would have made good fighting-companions—but those times, alas! are not now ..."

The two men looked steadily at each other; then Hugh O'Neill turned away with a short, disappointed laugh. "So be it ... even so, you are more than welcome to winter here under my protection, and return to Spain in the spring, when your injuries are healed, and the weather more certain—and who knows? Before then, I might even be able to convert you to my way of thinking....?" He sniffed the air, speculatively; again,

Miguel was reminded of a sly, powerful fox, ready to spring.... Then, as Don Alonso still shook his head, O'Neill made ready to ride off again, remarking with a chuckle that he had an appointment with the Governor of Ulster himself in a few days' time, and that after this talk he would be hard put to it to keep a straight face, when assuring the Englishman that he was doing all he could to capture every Spaniard straying into his territory!

"They're such fools, these English! Complacent, arrogant fools!" he burst out, bitterly. "They think they have made me one of them, because I have kissed Elizabeth's hand...but by the time I have finished, there'll not be one Englishman left alive throughout the length and breadth of Ireland! Tell your King that!"

"There goes a fanatic eaten up by hatred and ambition," said Don Alonso, thoughtfully. "I am not sure which I pity most—his acknowledged enemies or those he calls his friends. Oh—I do not doubt he loves his country—but he loves Hugh O'Neill most of all! It will not only be the English whom he makes suffer, when his revolt begins—as begin one day I am sure it will—but any of his fellow-Irishmen who happen to stand in his way..."

Next day, the Spaniards began boarding ship. The sick and injured, like Don Alonso, had to be winched up in improvised slings of nets and sailcloth, and it was evening before they were able to weigh anchor. Don Luis was smiling; Miguel tried to respond, and wished he could feel more cheerful. Were they not homeward bound, at last, after all? And yet...

To try to overcome his secret sense of foreboding, he cheered almost more loudly than anyone, as the great galleass moved majestically out into Donegal Bay, the sacred banners saved from the *Rata* and the *Duquesa*

Santa Ana flying proudly alongside her own. She was slow-moving and rather clumsy; "a floating castle", Hugh O'Neill had called her, disparagingly, built for the landlocked waters of the Mediterranean, not for the fickle Atlantic. Her gilded paintwork was faded and chipped; her ornate carvings smashed; the smallest wave set her creaking and shuddering ominously.

Everyone spent the night crammed tightly together on the open decks, hardly daring to move lest the slightest shift in weight on such an overloaded ship should start a chain-reaction to disaster. Don Alonso slept in his litter on the poop-deck; Miguel and his father huddled nearby.

For a while, Miguel struggled to keep awake, feeling, somehow, that if he did so he could keep all those dark, shameful fears he had from turning into any sort of reality. But it was no good; before very long he had fallen into a shallow, patchy sleep, his father's comforting words echoing in his ears: "Our nightmare is nearly over, God be praised! We can sleep easily tonight—and every night, from now on!"

But alas! The worst of the nightmare was yet to come.

Towards dawn, Miguel was awoken by the violent juddering of the deck beneath him. The fine October weather had broken suddenly and a gale from the southwest was now pushing the *Girona* nearer and nearer the northernmost tip of Ireland, with all its uncharted rocks and reefs. And, beneath the strain, the roughly-repaired rudder was beginning to give way!

All day, the seas grew higher; it began to rain, then to hail; and the hail froze on the decks, and the galleass sank still lower in the water. As darkness fell again, a few men panicked, and jumped over the sides, only to be sucked straight under the ship and drowned; then, as

96

ever bigger waves began breaking over the decks, others were swept overboard and drowned with them. But, in the main, Don Alonso's discipline held. The sodden, frozen men on the heaving decks kept their nerve, and, down below, the rowers battled grimly on.

A vivid flash of lightning streaked the sky; a dark, craggy land-mass appeared momentarily on the horizon. Don Alonso gave a shout of triumph. "Scotland! That's Scotland! Another hour or so—and all our troubles will be at an end!"

There were sighs of relief, even a few cheers; the prayers turned from supplications to thanksgivings. But at that moment, the last strands of rope holding the damaged rudder together finally parted; her steering gone, the galleass was at the complete mercy of the wind and the sea. Like a wounded whale, she began drifting helplessly shorewards—and though the rowers sweated and strained with the desperation of men who knew they were about to die, they could not alter her course...

Miguel gripped his father's hand; willing with all his might that with him, he was safe; they would come through, as they always had; drowning, dying, were things that only happened to other people.... After all, they had to get back to Almengo-Real, to Mother... *oh, Mother, I hope you are praying for us now, for I have forgotten every prayer I ever knew*, he thought hysterically, his mind a seething, feverish turmoil of fear... then he saw Father's lips moving, caught the familiar words he had said so often but which had never before been so real: *Holy Mary, Mother of God, pray for us sinners now and in the hour of our death....* He was saying them, over and over again, mingling them with appeals to every saint he knew, when the world heaved and spun and fell to pieces around him in a final awful shudder and a splinter of shattering timbers as the *Girona* struck a submerged rock, broke in half, and began to fill and sink.

Now Father was propelling him to the side of the galleass, heaving him on to the gunwhale. "Jump, Miguel—then swim for your life! The shore is not far off!" Don Luis' voice was calm and steady; Miguel was about to obey, unthinking, then came to his senses and arched back on to the deck again.

"I don't leave without you! We swim together!"

But Father was shaking his head. "My place is with Don Alonso. He is helpless—but you're a strong swimmer. I believe you will reach the shore alone! But hurry!"—as the broken ship began settling lower in the water. "There is not much time left!"

He was on the gunwhale again. Father said urgently: "Tell your mother how I loved her! And tell her I am sorry that——", but the rest of the sentence was lost, as Don Luis gave him a final push and he tumbled headlong into the bubbling icy water far below.

It seemed a lifetime before he surfaced, half-stunned by the cold and the force of his fall. All around him, a terrible, shrieking blackness. Slowly, his eyes grew accustomed to the darkness and he could see the greedy crests of the waves and the scores of men struggling in the water. People were shouting and screaming; spars, planks, barrels were tossing about all over the place. Men clung to them—or were knocked senseless by them. Miguel shouted vainly for his father. There was no response, and in his heart he knew even then that there never would be. His father and Don Alonso—a one-armed man helping a cripple—what hope had they? His mind registered the fact, unemotionally; only very much later, when feeling returned, would the full impact of it hit him.

He seemed to have been swimming for hours; his legs and arms were like heavy blocks of ice. At the start, there had been other swimmers round him, shouting, weeping, praying; but little by little the noise died away, and one by one the faces disappeared. Now he was all alone. He wondered why. He felt a fresh wave of fear as he wondered whether, after all, he had been swimming out to sea all this time, instead of towards land. It was so quiet—only the waves and the wind and no more human voices . . .

His knee jarred against something sharp; then there were rocks and seaweed under him. He stumbled shore-wards, falling back more than once into the waves. Suddenly there was firm sand beneath his feet; but then the cold seemed to overwhelm him, his legs refused to obey him any longer. The ground was opening beneath him, and he was falling . . . and terrified, he closed his eyes, for fear he was falling into Hell itself.

CHAPTER TEN

Trapped!

The waves roared in his ears; then he thought he heard his father shouting, and he began swimming towards the sound of his voice. But long before he reached him, Father had disappeared between the waves; Miguel had a vivid impression of his hand, with Mother's little heart-shaped gold ring on the index finger, slipping slowly from sight.... Everything seemed to be crowding in on him, swimmers, ships, all running him down; he struggled from the water and started to run up the beach. But the sand was soft, and soon he was sinking waist-deep in it, and as he fought to free himself a squadron of English cavalry came thundering towards him. He saw the bright flash of steel, waited, helpless, to be run through—only to find himself drenched instead in a soft, scented shower of orange-blossom, and with blessed relief he realized he was back at Almengo-Real, and that no danger could touch him any more...

So it went on, this series of images of people and places from the past; some repeating events exactly as they had happened, others frighteningly distorted, yet sometimes seeming the more real because of it. And, at the same time, these rapidly changing sensations of heat and cold, of raging thirst and vertigo...

Once or twice, the sequence broke, and he would glimpse something on an entirely different plane of existence. So he was dimly aware, at one point, of being dragged painfully up a steep, rocky incline, then pitched headfirst across the back of a donkey—the pungent smell of animal sweat and hair filled his nostrils.... Much later, a face stared down at him—a weather-beaten, wizened face, framed in a shock of white hair, the kindly grey eyes anxious and fearful. There was the glow of burning turf, the lowing of cattle, the stench of cow-dung...

Gradually, the fantasies faded; the old man's face became more intrusive. At last came the day when Miguel opened his eyes to find him trying to force a bitter-tasting liquid down his throat.

He spluttered in disgust and shut his eyes again. Then opened them. The man was still there—and smiling.

He heard his own voice, like some stranger's, little more than a croak: "My father—did you find him, too?"

But he knew, even as he spoke, that there could be but one answer to his question. The pain of it seemed almost too great to bear, and he shut his eyes, and drifted into unconsciousness again. Little by little, however, as the days passed, he became reconciled to the inevitable and was able to appreciate the miracle of his own survival. And, as he did so, the memory of those final terrifying hours on the *Girona* began to dim; he remembered, instead, all the good moments he and his father had shared. Strangely, in that last glimpse, as he urged Miguel to jump from the sinking galleass, Don Luis had become again to his son all that he had been in happier times—strong, decisive, self-assured—and perhaps it had not been simply the bewildering half-light of the storm that had made him seem, at the end, as handsome and debonair as long ago.

Now, at last, the final horror of their defeat and destruction penetrated his full consciousness. He wept, not just for his father, not just for those who had drowned on the *Girona*, but for all those thousands who would never see Spain again.

It had come to pass, exactly as the Irish bard had foretold. Sean had been right. But who else could have foreseen that it would all end like this—all those high hopes brought to nothing, dashed to pieces on the rocks of Antrim, or drowned forever beneath the grey Atlantic! The flower of Spain had perished on that black night of October 26th—Don Alonso, the pattern of Spanish chivalry, and with him, the sons of almost every great house in the land. And with them, also, score upon score of humble men who had come on this great expedition simply at their landlords' bidding— let alone the galley-slaves who had had even less choice in the matter. Many of them, brought forcibly on this modern Crusade, had not even been Christians...

As Miguel grew stronger he began to take in his new surroundings. He was lying on a bed of soft bracken on the sandy floor of a cave; he knew he must still be very near the sea, for he could clearly hear in the middle distance the constant pounding of the waves from which the old cowherd had rescued him. Beyond the entrance to the cave was a sweet green pasture. Each day, the cowherd would graze his cattle there, returning two or three times during the daylight hours to ply Miguel with soured milk and berries and oatcakes, and, in the evening, bringing all his cows and even his donkey into the cave to sleep. In the glow of the peat fire, he and Miguel would stare at one another, each sizing the other up. Neither could speak the other's language; they communicated by drawing pictures in the sand on the cave floor.

So Miguel tried to sketch out Almengo, and his

family, and soon he came to learn that this solitary old man had once had a wife and son of his own, but that they were now long dead; the cowherd pointed to the stars beyond the cave, smiling wistfully, and crossed himself. He knew they were in Heaven, and he no longer mourned. Sometimes Miguel wondered if perhaps it was the memory of that dead son that had led the cowherd to risk his life in bringing him up from the rocks and nursing him back to health as he had done. The sight of this kind, lonely old man was infinitely comforting; it made Miguel realize, really for the first time in his life, that other people could suffer grievous losses too—and still survive.

So the days drifted by, almost pleasantly; time seemed to have lost all meaning. As to the future, Miguel had blotted that from his mind.

Then, one morning, Miguel awoke to find the turf fire cold and dead, and the cowherd and his cattle quite vanished. On the floor beside him was a bowl of soured milk, a pile of oat bannocks, and the cowherd's own thick plaid cloak. They were the only signs of a farewell that Miguel realized was utterly final. The cowherd had concluded that he was well enough, now, to fend for himself, and had moved on with his cows to pastures new.

It took Miguel some time to take in fully what had happened; that he was now quite alone. His immediate reaction was one of indignation. That was soon succeeded by a mounting panic. How would he be able to manage, on his own? How would he be able to keep himself alive in this strange, enemy land—let alone escape from it? The cowherd had no right to slip away and leave him like this!

Then he grew calmer and began to see the situation in better perspective. He recalled, with gratitude, that the

old cowherd had after all saved his life, risking his own
to do so; indeed, he could not have expected to go on
being protected forever. Now he was well again, he
must learn to stand on his own feet. He had survived
when all the odds had been against him, and when so
many had perished; now, somehow, he must find a way
of escaping from this terrible country, where horror
seemed to succeed horror, of getting back to Spain, to
Almengo...

But how? Shakily, he made his way to the entrance
to the cave and peered cautiously out. It was something
he had never attempted to do while the cowherd was
caring for him; then, cocooned in sympathy, the outside
world had ceased to have any importance. Now all
that was abruptly changed.

Ahead of him lay the green sweep of the cliffs, falling
sharply away, with the sea behind them. And, further
along the cliffs, seeming about to topple headlong into
the waters below it, a great, frowning pile of a building
which clearly belonged to someone extremely powerful.

Miguel shuddered involuntarily: such a castle must
surely be an English strong-point! And he stumbled
back into the cave, as if afraid someone could see him
from those distant windows.... Then he remembered.
This was Ulster, after all. The country of Hugh O'Neill
and of other Irish chieftains who still had real power of
their own. Perhaps this fortress was the home of an
Irish lord, who, like O'Neill, hated the English, and
would help him escape to Scotland?

Then he started, as the sound of voices drifted up
from the beach below, and he felt the sweat breaking
out on his forehead and saw that his hands were shaking.
Were there English soldiers searching these shores for
him, and people like him? But even as he listened,

trembling, he caught the lilting inflections and knew that the people he could hear were talking Gaelic, and so must be Irish.

Slowly, wriggling along the grass on his stomach, he edged his way to the cliff-edge and peered over. He caught his breath, appalled. He must be almost opposite the place where the *Girona* had sunk. The whole beach here was swarming with fierce, heavily-armed Irishmen, crawling over the rocks, hauling away the wreckage—timbers, cannon, handfuls of gold and silver coins—enriching themselves on the spoils of dead men ... those pieces of eight might have been his father's.... He felt suddenly giddy and sick, and stumbled, retching, back into his hideout. All the bitter memories from the past came flooding back to him, and once more he was overwhelmed by the hopelessness of his own situation.

All that day Miguel sat stunned in the cave, reliving yet again those last hours on the *Girona*. And when dusk finally came, and he fell into an exhausted sleep, he dreamt he was following his mother down the passageways at Almengo, begging her to turn and look at him, and see that he was alive. But she only murmured that he had been drowned, long since, with his father. When she put out her hand to touch him, it passed right through him, indicating that what she said was true, that he was no more than a ghost ...

He awoke, bathed in sweat, shouting. But there was no one to hear.

Dawn was just breaking; now at least he knew what he was going to do. He *must* get back to Almengo, and no amount of sentiment could be allowed to stand in the way. Those Irishmen he had seen on the beach yesterday would have come from the castle, he was sure of it, for there was no other building in sight; and that meant that whoever owned the castle was greedy for

Spanish gold. Somehow Miguel did not imagine he would be the sort of person who would offer help freely, as the poor Irish, from Sean to the cowherd, had done; this man would demand payment. How better to pay him than in this same Spanish gold and silver of which he was so fond? If Irishmen could search for Spanish *reales* and pieces of eight from the wreck, then so could he! And, even if they were coins which had once belonged to his father or his father's friends—sombrely, he crossed himself—he was certain that they would only approve his action in taking them now.

Buoyed up with new hope, he slipped out of the cave, followed the cliff until he came to a steep path that dropped down to the beach, and gingerly made his way on to the sands.

By the time the sun was high in the sky, his back was aching and his fingers bruised and bleeding from poking among the rocks and shingle. But he had already found a dozen or so gold coins! Tremendously elated, he felt as though he were halfway back to Spain already! So absorbed was he in his search that he never noticed the file of yesterday's Irishmen wending their way down the cliff towards him; the first he knew was when one of them seized him by the scruff of the neck, pinioned his hands behind him, and lashed them expertly together with a rope.

Even in his stunned surprise, he was not totally disheartened; this was all a stupid misunderstanding, after all—once the owner of the castle knew who he was and what he wanted, everything would be all right. . . . This mood of optimism stayed with him most of the way to the castle itself. But as he drew nearer, it began first to waver, then died altogether.

At close hand, the castle looked grimmer and gloomier than ever. There were more armed Irishmen, like those he had encountered on the beach, sauntering in the dirty, rubbish-strewn courtyard, but there were other armed men there, too—soldiers—and *English* soldiers at that!

Miguel almost fainted with terror. But then he noticed that neither English nor Irish seemed to be having anything to do with one another; they were merely sharing the same building. And none of the English took the least interest in him; to them, he was simply some Irish lad in trouble with his fellow-countrymen. Perhaps the great man who held this castle was indeed another Hugh O'Neill; apparently tolerating, even liking the English, but secretly against them. Or so Miguel tried to comfort himself.

Then he was pushed into a great, dark room, lit with candles, although it was daylight outside; and pushed so hard that he stumbled and fell to the stone floor and had difficulty in rising again because of the rope binding his hands. All the while, the Irishmen—for this room was filled with more of these ferocious-looking people —laughed at his efforts. A flush of shame took away some of his terrified pallor.

Seated in a high-backed chair, surrounded by his retainers, was a diminutive, elderly figure of a man, tightly wrapped in a plaid cloak, even though the room was heated by a massive peat fire, and Miguel felt the atmosphere stiflingly hot. One gnarled hand drummed on the arm of his chair; from out of a heavily-lined, sunken face there peered eyes as grey as the cowherd's —but these were not kind, sad eyes, but avaricious, cruel and suspicious.

A torrent of Gaelic was directed at Miguel; he understood not a word, but he knew instinctively that it was not friendly. As he shook his head, the old man beckoned to a figure in the background—a man seeming more timid and self-effacing than the rest.

He began speaking, in Latin, and then Miguel realised he must be the old man's priest, and his hopes rose a little again—then fell, as the priest pointed to the gold coins on the table—the ones that Miguel himself had found.

"You are in Antrim, the land of Somhairle Buidhe McDonnell," he began—"And all the wreckage which is found on this coast belongs to him! The penalty for taking what is rightly his is death! Did you not know that?"

Stumbling a little—for his Latin was hesitant for lack of use, and he was very frightened—Miguel tried to explain. He told how he had been wrecked in the *Girona*, had taken shelter—and had collected the coins from his own father's ship because he intended using them to buy a passage to Scotland—and safety. Now he was begging for mercy. "Many Irish people helped us in our struggle to get back to Spain!" he cried, desperately. "Will you not help me now? I have heard that Ireland as well as Spain is the enemy of England! And I promise you—when I reach Spain again—my family will see you are well rewarded in gold—" he tried to draw himself up, to maintain some semblance of dignity despite his bonds—"for we are not paupers! My father headed one of the greatest families in Spain and we do not lack riches!"

As this was translated a glint appeared momentarily in the old man's eye, and Miguel sensed he found the offer tempting. But, even as he watched the old man spoke again, coldly, and, once more, Miguel's hopes faded. "The McDonnell does not believe you would keep your promise to repay him, even if you really do possess these riches you speak of—" and, even as Miguel tried to protest—"Besides, what you ask is out of the question. This family has indeed had its share of bloody quarrels with the English, but all that is past, now. There is a truce between us. They let us go our own way—and in return, we cause them no trouble. It is a fair bargain. True enough—not long ago, The McDonnell showed great kindness and helped the five other men who survived your wreck—we all thought there were but five, and none of them was of much significance—to reach Scotland. The McDonnell is not an unmerciful man. But, as far as you are concerned—" the priest's hands fluttered, and Miguel realized he did not relish what he was saying, but, since he was just a chaplain, a McDonnell retainer like the rest, he had no choice—"that is impossible. A few weeks ago, the situation was very different, there were no Englishmen here to ask questions. Now, we have an English garrison within our walls, and the Governor of Ulster himself is staying in this castle—it is far too dangerous for us to help you. We need his friendship above all else! So, my son—" and now the priest was mumbling in his embarrassment, talking so rapidly that Miguel could scarcely follow his words—"Although we could punish you ourselves for stealing what is ours—we intend to send you to the Governor, instead, as an earnest of our good intentions towards him and his. Let *him* deal with you!"

CHAPTER ELEVEN

The Englishman

Events moved swiftly, after that. Miguel was taken back to the courtyard, and handed over ceremonially to an English captain, his former Irish escort smiling and bowing obsequiously, while the priest interpreted. Miguel felt sick to the stomach with the hypocrisy of it all, so shocked and disgusted that for a few minutes he almost forgot to be afraid.

But the deadening panic, the cold fear, soon returned. For now a couple of English soldiers were leading him up flights of steep stone steps and along murky, winding passages, until Miguel's sense of direction boggled. All the time his brain was racing, feverishly ... there must be something he could do to avert the horror ahead of him—but what?

He remembered both the Donegal priest and Hugh O'Neill remarking that the Governor of Ulster was not like Bingham of Connaught—had not O'Neill declared, mockingly: *The English have given us a Governor who is a gentleman*! So perhaps this man would be prepared to free him, against a ransom which Miguel knew his Sanchez grandfather would be only too willing to pay—the traditional practice, regarding prisoners-of-war, after all.... But, on reflection, this hardly seemed likely. The English were not taking any prisoners this time. The McDonnells, he felt sure, had handed him over as a prize well worth the killing!

Well, it would soon be over, now. He braced himself

to die as a Spaniard should, as bravely as his own father had done. For they had stopped at last outside a heavy, studded door, flanked by English guards. The door swung open; Miguel was marched inside.

The room was as grey and drab as the rest of the castle, with one single splash of colour—the red and white flag of England, which Miguel remembered so vividly from the days of the sea-battles, hung on one wall. Beneath it, a man was seated at a long oak table, writing. He was wearing a breastplate; his helmet and sword lay on the table beside his papers; otherwise there was nothing especially awe-inspiring about Captain Christopher Carleill. Someone less terrified than Miguel would have been more impressed by his weariness; the fair hair on the bent head was faded and thinning, the clothes heavily travel-stained.

The soldiers loosed Miguel's bonds, saluted, uttered a few sentences of explanation, and withdrew. The door slammed behind them.

There was silence; except for the pen scratching monotonously across the paper, and the sound of the waves, crashing against the cliffs below the window. After what seemed to Miguel an eternity, the Governor leaned back in his chair and looked thoughtfully at the ragged figure before him. Then he spoke, reasonably enough at first, and in Spanish.

"You say you come from the *Girona*, and that you are the Count of Almengo-Real's son," he said. "But it is more than six weeks, now, since the *Girona* sank. Someone must have been sheltering you during those six weeks ... and I need to know who that person is!" And, as Miguel hesitated, he rapped out, sharply: "Withholding information now can do you nothing but harm—and, you must know, your situation could hardly be more desperate!"

Miguel hung his head, utterly defeated. Then he remembered the old cowherd; the many kindnesses of those past weeks in the cave by the sea blotted out the bitter memories of the meeting with the McDonnell chieftain. For people like the cowherd, at least, it was still worth fighting...

"I do not even know the name of the person who helped me!" he retorted. "—Except—" bitterly—"it cannot have been McDonnell! And even if I did know it I would not tell you. I only know that whoever took me in did it out of simple goodness—he was poor, and alone, and of no consequence, and, God forgive me, in my days at home in Spain I would have passed him by and not noticed him...but he rescued me out of pure compassion, and nursed me back to health—for you to kill!" Miguel stamped his foot, carried away by the sheer force of his argument now, not caring what he said. "I will never tell you who or what he was, I swear it, no matter what you do to try to make me! He did nothing wrong—unless you call it wrong to help another human being in trouble——" and he flushed, suddenly horrified by the candour of his own words, and yet, at the same time, in his heart of hearts, convinced that he had rarely spoken with more sincerity and truth than he was speaking now.

But the Englishman was smiling. "I think I should tell you now that the official penalty for harbouring a Spaniard is death," he said, almost mildly. "But I shall press you no further. It can serve no useful purpose. Besides," he went on, "I am glad to see that Spaniards still have some spirit!—As they had, when I learned my Spanish, fighting your countrymen in the Americas, many years ago...but things were different, then." He shrugged, sadly. "I think that although I am not yet forty, I am growing old, and begin to tire of

living. Perhaps, after all, I was not cut out for soldiering
—certainly, these last weeks in Ireland have sickened me
out of mind.... Believe me," he said, leaning forward
earnestly— "it grieves me beyond measure to think of
so many brave men perishing as your companions have
done—so uselessly—for—" and he looked at Miguel
very hard—"You realize that you never could have
succeeded in your venture, do you not? Even had you
managed to land in England, you would never have
conquered us! Your Armada was doomed before it
started!"

For a moment, Miguel did not reply; then,
reluctantly, he murmured: "I think we all knew that,
by the end—my father certainly did, and it broke his
heart, after all his high hopes, and I really believe now
that Don Alonso knew it even before we set out from
Lisbon—but there was nothing we could do—because
the King had ordered it...."

"Exactly!" The Governor banged his fist on the table
so that the papers there shivered and shook. "The King
ordered it! And so you all obeyed! Just as the Queen of
England has ordered the execution of every Spaniard
who sets foot in Ireland! And—in the same way—*her*
subjects obey *her*...also without question...." His
voice faltered; then he added, uncertainly, almost as if
to himself: "But I for one have never before been
ordered to kill defenceless prisoners! I always prided
myself that such atrocities were committed only by the
armies of other nations! I never thought to see my own
fellow-countrymen, like the Binghams, revelling in
cold-blooded murder!"

He stood up, seeming suddenly to have made up his
mind at last, and to be casting off a great burden. "I
ought to send you to the Lord Deputy," he murmured,
"But my conscience cries out against it! The last Spanish

prisoners I sent him—men who had surrendered to me of their own free will—were returned, with a message, telling me to hang them all forthwith! But I could not do it—so I packed them off to Scotland.... I'm a Christian, as well as an Englishman, and it is no part of my duty to campaign against the helpless.... In any case, I came to Dunluce this week to try to extract the *Girona's* treasure from these double-dealing McDonnell freebooters, here, not to hunt fugitives—I leave that to those with more taste for the task! Your capture came about by sheer chance. The McDonnells seized upon it as a heaven-sent opportunity to ingratiate themselves with me—hoping, no doubt, that I should deal more tolerantly with them in consequence.... This is a blood-stained land, full of contradictions, and no one should envy us the task of trying to bring some semblance of order into it." Then he smiled, faintly. "When villains like Somhairle Buidhe, the McDonnell chieftain, and Hugh O'Neill can trick and cheat the Queen at every turn and still be considered loyal—who am I to know who is dangerous and who is not!... So you will stay here, under guard, until nightfall. When it is dark, I shall have you put aboard a fishing-boat for Scotland——"

At first, Miguel could scarcely believe the Governor's words; it was like a miracle, too wonderful to be real. But when he tried to stammer out his thanks, the Englishman refused to listen, and till the guard came to take him away, he was very cool and formal again, Miguel's idea of the typical Englishman once more, turning back to his papers, leaving Miguel standing, not knowing what to say next.

As he was marched off, Miguel promised, "You have my word on it—when I reach Spain, my family will send you a fine ransom——"

But the Governor of Ulster shook his head. "I want no ransom. It is as I told you—I am growing old, and seeing things too clearly for comfort any more. Only remember, Miguel, when you tell your children and your children's children tales of the cruel and unfeeling English, that you once met one of them, at least, who was foolish enough to show mercy...."

CHAPTER TWELVE

Home-coming

At dusk, he was taken down the cliff by an armed escort, and transferred to a tiny cockle-shell of a fishing-boat. Miguel caught his breath; the waves seemed so large and this boat so small; how could it possibly cross a stretch of sea that had defeated the great *Girona*?

But already, the soldiers were pushing him towards it. He saw one of them toss a purse of coins to the skipper. The soldiers turned away, up the cliff. The boat cast off. He would be in Scotland before daybreak.

Miguel crouched down for warmth in the bottom of the boat, glad of the rough homespun cloak which one English soldier had given him; grateful, too, for the food which the Governor had sent him before he left the castle. He watched its gaunt outline growing smaller and smaller as they moved out to sea. There was a light still shining from one of the topmost windows; he was almost certain that it was in that very room that the Englishman had interrogated him. Perhaps he was there now, working far into the night on his papers; perhaps he was even looking out, watching Miguel set off on the escape which his humanity and generosity alone had made possible.

Miguel remembered Sean's gruesome stories of the Governor of Connaught; of how he had slaughtered hundreds upon hundreds of helpless Spaniards in cold blood. Here in Ulster, it had been very different. Instead of killing his prisoner, this Governor had given

him food, clothes, even set him on a boat to Scotland—
his passage paid for out of his own pocket! So many
terrible things had happened, over the past months,
that the world had come to seem to Miguel a harsh and
cruel place, and many of the people in it, harsh and
cruel too. But now one man's actions shone out like a
radiant light, a bright, redeeming force, and suddenly
the evil which had seemed so overwhelming lost some
of its power . . .

On the west coast of Scotland, where he was landed,
there were still people sympathetic to the Spanish cause,
and eager to help him. Miguel found shelter there till
the worst of the winter storms were over; then, when
the snow began to melt, he took ship for Spain.
By the time the long sea voyage ended at the Seville
quayside, it was already spring. News of Miguel's safe
return had travelled ahead of him; his grandfather was
waiting to greet him as he stepped back on to the soil
of Spain. He knelt on the cobbles at the water's edge,
stroking the dirty stones as if they were precious
diamonds. He was half-afraid, even now, that he might
be dreaming; that the blue river and bluer sky, the
sparkling white buildings and the familiar faces might
turn out, after all, to be nothing but a mirage; and
that he might yet wake to find himself back in the
icy Atlantic, on the night of the *Girona's* sinking, the
screams of the drowning echoing all around him . . .
But his grandfather was real enough, not much
changed—a little greyer, perhaps—but smiling now as
tears of happiness rolled down his wrinkled cheeks.
Miguel stepped forward to embrace him, remembering
with renewed shame that it was his grandfather's
fortune which had been used to finance his and Father's
part in an enterprise of which his grandfather had

disapproved from the start. "I am truly sorry," he muttered, filled with a sense of his own inadequacy. "We failed—utterly—and now everything is lost...."

His grandfather shrugged his shoulders philosophically, and continued smiling. "Not everything. *You* are alive, thank God—and now Almengo-Real can come back to life again, too. For since you and your father went away, your mother has not really lived at all... now you can change all that."

Can I? thought Miguel, wretchedly. I have come back, but not Father. How can I ever begin to make up for all that she has lost?...*If my love alone could protect you, you would truly be invincible*, his mother had declared. Alas, she had not known, then, that those were the last words she would ever say to her husband. And, in the end, all the love in the world had not been able to mend his shattered faith in himself, nor yet to save him from a nameless, watery grave, far, far away, off the cold, desolate coast of Ireland.... Somewhere, on the ocean floor, there must lie now that little gold ring with its engraved lovers' message. Miguel prayed that it, at least, would never find its way into Somhairle Buidhe McDonnell's greedy coffers! Better that it stay forever at the bottom of the sea—for how could anyone finding it understand even a fraction of what it had meant to the two people who had given and received it?

He was determined to start back for Almengo-Real straight away, declining the splendid feast which had been prepared for him in Seville—refusing even to stop and change the drab serge he had worn since Scotland for any of the fine selections of silks and velvets spread out for him to choose from.

"Mother will be waiting for me," he explained to his grandfather. "And besides—" his mouth quivered, and he felt again that overwhelming bitterness and grief—"I am hardly coming home victorious. There is no point in pretending that this is some kind of triumphal procession."

"So be it." Grandfather nodded. "Even so," he went on, gently but firmly, "you cannot brood on the past forever. Here in Spain we have been in mourning since the summer. Surely, it is time now to look to the future. Can we not be grateful that you at least have come back, after all hope had gone—and that the castle has a master, once more?"

Of course, Grandfather was right. All the same, as the little procession made its way slowly along the winding Almengo road, it was hard not to be overcome by memories of that triumphant procession from the *castle*, along this same road, only a year ago—and with every mile they went, it became even harder. Then, he had been a child; in that year, he had grown up—but at what cost! Then, he and Father had been setting out for Lisbon, with the world at their feet—he remembered so well the banners, the flowers, the bells, the cheering crowds—and Father's rapturous predictions of still greater rejoicing on the return that was to have been so glorious!

There was no cheering this time. But men and women still rushed up to Miguel, grasping his hand, crying, "Long life and happiness, my lord," and then, crossing themselves, "and may your father's soul rest in peace!" Only rarely was there any direct reference to the events of the past year; as when someone called out, encouragingly, "Never fear, my lord—we'll sweep these English scum off God's earth yet!"

Miguel winced. "But for an Englishman—I should not be here today!" he retorted, sharply—but what was the use? How could anyone who had not been through it all, ever understand?

The last half-mile was the hardest of all to bear. It was afternoon, now; *siesta*-time; the countryside slept under the April sun. The new foliage on the olives glimmered like spun silver; the first clusters of starry blossoms were bursting on the lemon trees. On such a day as this, the *siesta* had been broken by Don Luis, returning so full of hope and excitement from Madrid, up this same path ... it was incredible, how everything looked just as it had then—when, in reality, so much had changed!

The standard of the Counts of Almengo-Real broke from the watch-tower; the signal that the riders had been sighted, and that a welcome awaited them.

"I did not want that!" Miguel protested, but his grandfather laid his hand on his arm.

"It has to be so. The Count is dead—yet long live the Count!" he said, steadily. "Your mother has accepted it, Miguel. For her sake, if not for your own, so must you!"

Miguel nodded dumbly. Life had to go on; and, indeed, as he knew in his heart, it still held much that was good and noble; the memory of those many kindnesses he had received over the past year—so unexpected, and the more wonderful because of it—the generosity of Sean and his peasants, the simple goodness of the poor cowherd, the mercy shown him by Christopher Carleill, the English Governor of Ulster—all these things sustained him now, and made him conscious that all was not completely lost, that a future lay ahead of him, and that he owed it to his past to make that future one of hope and promise.

Now they were passing under the archway. Beyond it, the courtyard was crowded with people, eager to greet the boy who, when all hope had been abandoned, had returned, so it seemed, from the very gates of death.

Miguel slid from his horse, glanced apprehensively at the assembled faces, their expressions a confusion of sympathy and curiosity...

A little to one side, stood a silent row of black-gowned, black-veiled women and girls—the widows, mothers and daughters of all the men who had set out from Almengo with Don Luis and, like him, had not returned. And Miguel remembered his father's tortured words in Killybegs: "*I dragged them into this, Miguel, I misled them with tales of glory and easy victory. But for my lunatic day-dreams they would all be alive now ... you must see to it, above all, that their dependants are provided for ...*"

Even as Miguel hesitated, overcome by his memories and his knowledge of endless obligation, one of the women stepped out from the rest and swept him a deep, graceful curtsey.

"Welcome to the fifteenth Count of Almengo-Real!" she cried, clearly and proudly, even though there was a tremble in her voice, and her face was wet with tears.

Then, at last, there were cheers, but Miguel did not hear them. He was rushing to lift his mother to her feet, to throw his arms around her, marvelling at how frail and tiny she had suddenly become. Though she was still very beautiful, the hair that had been jet black a year ago had turned quite white.

"How tall you have grown!" she exclaimed. "And you walk so firmly, now—why, for a moment, I almost believed it was your father!"

He would have done anything, then—gone back to being just a slight, timid boy with a limp and no confidence in himself—to have been able to turn back the clock.

"It should have been so different!" he burst out, full of renewed bitterness, "If only——"

But his mother was shaking her head. "It was God's

will," she said, quietly. "I only thank Him that He spared you for me——"

What nonsense, Miguel longed to shout—if I have learned anything from this past year, it is that God does not take sides—*He* does not will the thousands upon thousands of futile deaths in battle and the like, even when they are fought in His name... each time men tear one another apart He suffers some sort of fresh Crucifixion.... No, it was better ships, better guns, better strategy that defeated us, not Divine Providence...

He looked down at his mother's face. Despite all that had happened, it was serene, even content. Like the rest of Spain, she had found a kind of comfort in this belief that God had willed their failure, and all the tragedies that had sprung from it—just as the English, in their turn, were declaring that He had deliberately intervened to give them the victory.... Who was he to destroy the illusion that supported her?

So, older and very much wiser than a year ago, he did not answer, but simply took her arm, and, as his father would have done, led the way into the castle.

AFTERWORD

Hugh O'Neill of Tyrone, the Irish lord who asked the Spaniards to help him foment a rebellion against the English, finally led a revolt in 1595. The uprising was a savage one, and not all the Irish joined him. Spanish help was too little and came too late. Eventually he was defeated, and he died in exile in Rome. Ulster was then largely settled by people from England and Scotland.